DANGEROUS

MADE & BROKEN I

NORA ASH

MIRA

It's not often I struggle to keep my professional facade when I'm with a patient, but today... today it was really, really difficult.

"I think this is the first time a bird's asked me to lie down while my clothes are still on."

I did my best to fight back the heat in my cheeks as my patient flopped down on the couch in my office with all the self-assuredness of a rockstar.

He looked like one too, with his black leather jacket and hard rows of muscles pressing against his t-shirt. It was white, and tight enough that I could see the shadow of several tattoos on his chest.

"Again, I didn't ask you to lie down. The couch is for deeper therapy—not the first evaluation."

He gave me a smirk and casually kicked his boot-clad feet up onto the armrest of the couch closest to me, lifting his arms above his head so his shirt stretched taut across his chest. "Is that so, Miss Holler?"

"Yes, that is so." I bit the inside of my cheek to keep my tone neutral while I stared at his face. His completely perfect face, with its high cheekbones, light gray eyes, and eyebrows raised in obvious mockery. His stupidly sensual mouth with its defined cupid's bow and full lower lip was drawn into an imitation of a smile, but the coolness in his almost silvery eyes contradicted it. Despite having scheduled an appointment with me himself, it was obvious that my newest patient saw me as an opponent to conquer.

I sighed and tried to relax my expression before it betrayed my inner turmoil. He might be a smart arse—with abs that looked like they were carved from rock, even through his clothes—but it was my job to help him. Even if I mostly just wanted to kick his arse off my couch and out the door for rattling me so thoroughly within five minutes of meeting him.

"Why are you here?"

The corner of his mouth slipped down for the briefest moment as his gaze flickered to his boots. A display of uncertainty? Interesting.

Then he looked back up, and his armor of arrogance was back, complete with that annoying smirk. "Never did do a psychologist before, and when I came across your name it reminded me of a stern schoolteacher. The prissy types always did it for me."

I counted silently to ten and wished that the blush I could feel spread across my face would go the hell away. "I very much doubt that's the case—"

"Your glasses are pretty hot. I wouldn't mind if you kept them on."

"—so how about you stop acting like a hormonal adolescent and tell me what's happened to make you seek out therapy?" I was pretty proud of how unwavering I managed to keep my voice, despite his interruption.

"And what if you're wrong and that *is* why I'm here?" With a single, graceful movement, the rockstar look-alike sat up and swiveled around so he was supporting his elbows on his knees. He leaned forward a little and focused his unnerving gaze on me, and his smirk hiked up a little at the corner. "Then what do we do?"

I suppressed a primal shiver at the almost predatory gleam in his eyes. No doubt he was used to women tossing their panties at him after being on the receiving end of that look—even *I* couldn't help the small burst of desire it made trickle through my abdomen, and I was already distinctly unimpressed with his bad boy routine.

"Then we have a very disappointing hour ahead of us, *Mr. Steel,* because that isn't happening. If that were truly your intent, then your money would have been better spent on one of the ladies down on the corner. Even if they charge extra for role playing, I'm sure you could have gotten it cheaper than what this session will cost you. Now, are you quite done trying to intimidate me so we can get on with the session?"

His smirk turned to a slow, full smile. "Mr. Steel now, is it? You can call me Blaine, love. My mother went out of her way to give me a, *ah,* special name, so you may as well use it."

"Do you have some resentment toward your mother?" I'm not gonna lie—I latched on to the mother angle with both hands.

"Nah, she was a good woman." Blaine pushed his fingers through his black, perfectly tousled hair and sighed.

"You say was? When did she die?"

He quirked an eyebrow at me. "Caught on to that one, eh? When I was ten, so about eighteen years ago now."

Finally. I'd found the crack in Blaine Steel's armor. "How did she die?"

Blaine frowned, his idling hand sliding from his hair down to the back of his neck. "Doesn't matter. It's a long time ago."

It was a clear dismissal. Everything from his tone to his suddenly darkening eyes told me that here lay trouble—which of course meant I needed to dig deeper. But as I'd pointed out to him before, this was just the initial consultation, where I was meant to learn more about a new patient before deciding on how to best proceed.

"Tell me a bit about the rest of your family. Your father. Siblings, if you have any."

He sighed again, as if relieved to leave the subject of his mum's death, and leaned back, arms spread out over the back of the sofa. "There's not much to tell. My dad's a strong leader, runs his business with an iron fist. He eventually remarried, and me and my five brothers joined the family business when we grew up."

He wasn't telling me even close to the truth. I narrowed my eyes at him and pushed my glasses up higher on my nose. I'd always been pretty good at reading body language, which is partly why I chose to study psychology in the first place, and Blaine was easy to read. Tensed shoulders, jaw slightly lifted in challenge, and a hard look in his gray eyes—yeah, he was hiding some major family drama.

"Why are you here, Blaine?" I kept my tone as light and gentle as I could, knowing that if I pushed too hard, he'd probably shut down, and I'd get treated to the delightful return of the cocky bastard who'd first sauntered into my small office.

"Shit, I don't know." He flexed his hands and leaned forward again, grabbing his knees as if looking for some anchor. The tension vibrating off him was practically palpable. "My brother went to jail and it was really fucked up. He didn't do shit, and I found out... I lost control. I nearly killed..." He looked up then, and straight into my eyes, and the torment in his gaze nearly knocked the breath out of my lungs.

It lasted for maybe a fifth of a second.

I could practically *see* the emotional wall slamming down the moment he realized he'd let me get even a sneak peak into whatever pain had made him desperate enough to seek out a therapist. Every part of his body tensed just a fraction, even as his face slid into a sardonic smile.

"Blaine..."

He let his gaze slide lazily up and down my body. "But then again, sometimes losing control is good. Isn't it, love?"

I gritted my teeth. I had been so close to seeing something real, but here we were, back to the arrogant bastard from before. It was funny, really. I'd known him for all of twenty minutes, and I was already sure that if I'd met him under any other circumstance than as a patient, I would not have walked away—I would have run. But he *was* my patient, and it was my duty to try to help him as best I could.

"You're using sexual innuendos to avoid talking about what's bothering you. I'm sure it's worked well for you so far, but let's for a minute assume you came here because something happened that was so bad, you didn't know what else to do. I know your type—you believe your masculinity lives in your ability to intimidate others and to never, ever show any hint of emotion. I *get* that being here goes against everything you've been brought up to believe in.

"So I guess the only question left is—was whatever happened to make you seek out professional help so bad you're willing to surrender all that attitude for what's left of our session?"

I was treated to what was quite obviously a rare sight—an array of emotions crossing Blaine Steel's handsome face, morphing from shock, frustration and finally into anger—until his eyes narrowed ever so slightly and his expression slid into the now familiar mask of irreverence. Only this time, there was an unmistakable edge of irritation behind his stare.

With the same ease as a big cat, he got up from the couch and strolled to the far wall where my diploma hung above a low bookshelf, back turned. "Attitude? Is that psychology-speak, then? I see you got your diploma at Liverpool John Moores University. Not exactly Stanford, is it?"

Despite myself, I felt my temper rise. If there was one thing in my life I was proud of, it was that I'd managed to overcome my fucked up past and acquire a degree that allowed me to help people.

"It's a hell of a lot better than being a petty thief, or whatever you did instead of educating yourself."

I shouldn't have let him get to me. And I especially shouldn't have lashed out—not only because it was as unprofessional as it got, but also because that was exactly what Blaine wanted. I saw it in his eyes the moment he turned back around, smug triumph written all over his stupidly handsome face.

"My, they do certainly educate quality shrinks up north, huh, love?" He walked over to my chair, all swagger, and it just made my blood boil all the more. "You'd think you at least were smart enough to keep your tongue in check. People have gotten hurt for a lot less than calling me a thief."

And there it was—the vocalization of the threat I'd seen in his eyes when I'd pushed him. No, he wasn't a thief. His cocky attitude stemmed from something much more sinister than that.

A burst of fear shot up my spine from that place deep inside where I had locked up all the horrible memories of what—and who—I came from.

This man was the same kind I had grown up with. The kind that took what they wanted and didn't shy away from using force to get it. Yeah, the kind of arrogance streaming off Blaine Steel was the kind a man attained when he was above the law.

He was dangerous.

The sudden spike of fear must have shown on my face, because some of the hardness in his gaze eased a little. He flicked his eyes up and down me again, then lowered his dark lashes halfway, focusing on my lips.

"Not that I'd hurt a bird—even if she is a mouthy little bitch."

His hand grazing gently across my cheek made my anger well up again, eradicating my fear in a smoldering flood of rage.

I smacked his hand away and flew to my feet. He was less than a foot away, and since I only came up to his shoulder, I had to crane my neck back to glare at him. "Get out."

There was no mistaking the victory in his eyes as he cocked an eyebrow at me with such self-assured arrogance that it took everything I had not to slap him. "You're really throwing me out of your office?"

"Yes, I am," I hissed. "And for the record, the next time you want someone to help you, you might get further if you show just an ounce of respect."

Blaine just smirked, obviously not the least bit bothered by my anger. "Respect, little dove, is not something I give out all that easily." And then he put his hand on my arse and squeezed. "But maybe you could try and win it another way?"

It was only that tiny voice of experience with men like Blaine at the back of my mind that stopped me from smacking the smirk off his face then and there. Instead, I stepped back and away from his touch so I could point at the door.

"Get. Out!"

TWO

MIRA

I have never been so thankful to reach the end of a work day as I was after my session with Blaine Steel.

I was still muttering to myself while I sorted out the last bit of paperwork so I could leave for the day. I could still feel the ghost of his hand against my backside, as if his touch had left a tingling sensation of awareness behind.

Which was partly why I was still angry. Not only had he made me completely lose my professional façade, but he'd also broken through all the walls surrounding my personal space and *touched* me. This arrogant prick, whom I'd loathed from the first moment I met, had put his hand on me.

And part of me had liked it.

I paused by the door and clutched at the knob as an echo of the shocking sensation of his hand against my arse made me shiver again. It shouldn't have felt good, *at all,* and I was furious at myself for having any sort of positive reaction to that... that *twat,* even if it was purely physical.

With a huff I turned the knob and yanked open the door. Clearly, it had been too long since I'd had a man in my life.

The irony wasn't lost on me. I'd gone to university to learn all about the human psyche, yet was unable to get past my own childhood trauma to let anyone properly into my life.

At least I acknowledged it. I locked my office door and put my keys into my purse with a sigh. Perhaps it was time to face my demons soon, so I could start looking for a good man without scaring him off like I had my last semi-serious boyfriend. If nothing else, then because it might stop my neglected ovaries from dancing on the tables just because a man with muscles and a wicked smile groped me.

It was dark when I stepped out of the run-down building and onto the street, as it always was this time of day in late October. Dim streetlights illuminated the pothole-rich road, but so many of them were busted that most of the light came from neon signs above closed shops, as well as the windows of the few restaurants and chippies lining the road. This part of East London wasn't exactly the poshest of places, but it was the only place I had been able to afford to set up my small office. I was situated just above a Thai restaurant. The thing about getting a new identity is that it makes it awfully hard to go to a bank and ask for a business loan.

"Hey, babe!"

I glanced up at a wolf-whistle, and then quickly looked straight ahead again at the sight of a small group of young men loitering by the corner shop. I'd seen them hang around the area before, but had always managed to cross the road before they spotted me. Too late now. The only thing worse than crossing the road after they'd seen me would be to turn around and run. I gritted my teeth and prepared myself for some inevitable harassment.

"What's you so uptight about, babe?" one of them shouted as I walked past without looking to their side.

"Bitch needs a good shag, mate," another said, which was followed by rough laughter. "Hey, come here, princess, and I'll show you what you need."

I ignored their shouts and rushed forward while clinging on to my purse, but suddenly, I found my way blocked.

One of the men had stepped out in front of me and was leering at me. "Calm down, babe. We just want to talk."

I tried to sidestep, but he followed and put a hand on my shoulder. "Not so fast."

My heart leapt into my throat at the contact. Catcalling and street harassment was one thing—a typical nuisance of being a single female out on her own

—but he was stopping me from leaving now, and I was having a hard time pushing back the first sliver of panic.

"Let go of me!"

"Aw, don't be like that," one of them purred behind me. "We just want to show you a good time."

"You should pay us for our kindness." A sharp tug on my purse's shoulder strap made me cling on harder to my bag.

"Get off me!"

"*Oi!* Leave the lady alone." It wasn't a full-on shout, but the new voice mixing in with the whoops and laughs of the group had a distinct no-nonsense tone. The guy grabbing on to my bag was shoved out of the way, and suddenly I was no longer alone in the circle of youths.

"Hey, who the fuck—" The protesting voice behind me died as the newcomer next to me spun around.

"Piss off. And if I see you harassing birds on the street again, you're going to regret the day you slid out of your mother's cunt, got it?"

Someone muttered "Sorry," and then, to my utter astonishment, they all took off down the street and around the corner.

I blinked and readjusted my purse, taking just a moment to gather myself before I looked up at my savior. "Thank you, that—" The words died in my throat when he turned around and his gray eyes met mine.

"You all right?"

"Yeah." I stared up at Blaine for a couple of seconds

—long enough for that trademark smirk to reappear— before I managed to pull myself together. "Why did they run from you like that?"

He shrugged and put both hands in his jean pockets. "My family's pretty well-known in some parts of the city. You headed for the station?"

I nodded and gave him a long side-look as he fell into step alongside me. In any big city, only a few families could make low-level thugs scarper just on sight. I'd made it a point to stay far, far away from those sorts of people since I left Belfast years ago, but there was no way Blaine knew anything about where I came from. If he had, I'd likely be in the back of a van by now, not casually strolling down the street beside him.

And, honestly, I was a bit curious as to what had made him come to my rescue.

"I didn't take you for the kind of guy who would lurk around, waiting for an opportunity to save damsels in distress."

Blaine laughed. "Haven't diagnosed me with a hero complex, then, little dove?"

"No—no, Mr. Steel, that I haven't. You are about as far from a hero as it gets."

"How rude," he hummed. "And after I swooped in and saved you from those big, bad bullies. Aren't therapists supposed to build up their patients' self-esteem?"

"Not when that patient's ego is already way overblown. But it's not like you'll be my patient going forward, so we're good regardless." Savior or not, being back in Blaine's presence and feeling my body instinctively lean toward him reminded me of how much of a jerk he'd been during our session. I scowled at his handsome profile for good measure.

"Does that mean you've changed your mind about shagging me?" He didn't even look at me, just grabbed my arm and stepped off the pavement so he could lead me across the road.

I did my best to ignore the shiver of awareness his touch drove through my skin, even through my wooly coat. Damn him and whatever all-male pheromones he seemingly bathed in before going out! And damn my traitorous ovaries.

"No offense, but I would rather slit my wrists." I yanked my elbow out of his grasp the moment we were on the pavement again. "Does this usually work for you? Do women really drop their knickers when you make your interest in their fun bits known?"

"Generally, they do, yes. In fact, your continued refusal might end up doing permanent damage to my fragile self-image. Isn't it in your ethical code that you must do what you can to help those who come to you seeking help? You really want to risk your professional reputation over the welfare of a patient?"

I really should have learned my lesson from our encounter in my office, but every word out of his mouth grated against my nerves—partly because of my frustration at my body's reactions, and partly because he served them with the most obscene smirk I'd ever seen. So instead of biting my tongue, I dug my heels in and rounded on him.

"I realize that your crippling self-hatred is so tied to your masculinity that you constantly try to undermine strong women with crude attempts at sexual dominance, but maybe you should try to see us as more than something to bury your cock in, hmm? Whatever it is you're so desperately trying to hide from yourself, it isn't going to go away by sexually harassing anyone who thinks to challenge you."

Blaine's deviant lips twitched, most likely at making me lose my temper—*again.* "Ah, but I have nothing against strong women, Miss Holler. I'll even let you be on top."

I took a deep—*deep*—breath and counted to ten. "Sometimes, *Blaine,* we don't get what we want. It's part of our emotional development. Clearly, you've missed out, so see this as an opportunity to better yourself. If I had gotten the pony I desperately wanted for my sixth birthday, I would probably have ended up a horrible human being who thought she could get anything and anyone she pointed at, as well." Yeah, I was subtle. "But I didn't, and look at me now, all capable of acting like a normal person."

My righteous fury had done nothing to dim the devilish gleam in Blaine's eyes. "You say I'm the one who's scared, but you should see yourself—you look positively terrified that a night in the sack with me will make that prim and proper façade of yours come tumbling down."

Well, ouch. That hit a tad too close to home. I took a step back and shook my head, disengaging as I should have done from the start. "I truly hope you learn to drop the bad boy act one day so you can get rid of your demons. Goodbye, Blaine."

I SPENT the train ride home doing my best to forget I'd ever met Blaine Steel, but it was hard to ignore how completely he'd gotten under my skin.

I knew it wasn't just because he'd made my panties damp. No, it was also because he reminded me so strongly of all the things I'd run away from, and all the things I still woke up from nightmares of. He was dangerous; there was no doubt in my mind about that after having looked into his eyes. He was the type of man who could and would crush a person if it suited him, and yet... I hadn't done everything I could to fly under the radar. I'd argued with him and shoved his flaws in his face, like some moron with a death wish.

Perhaps it meant that I was finally starting to heal? Maybe, if I could face a man like Blaine and not imme-diately turn around and run in the other direction, then my childhood had finally lost its petrifying grip on me.

I felt marginally better when I got off the train, but I was still too emotionally squashed to consider cooking.

I stopped by my local chippy on my way home, giving my current diet a remorseful thought as the bell jingled merrily upon my entry.

"Chicken Kung Pao, Mira?" Mr. Chang sent me a friendly smile when the smell of fried food and soy sauce enveloped me.

Okay, so maybe there was a reason I never really completed a diet, leaving me in an eternal cycle of restrictive eating, binging, and then guilt. When your local chippy knew both your name and your regular order, there weren't all that many excuses left.

"Yeah, thanks, Chang," I said, sending him a pale smile. "With extra sauce, please."

Oh well, the guilt would have to wait until tomorrow. Right now, all I wanted out of life was my Kung Pao, my sofa, and a date with *Doctor Who*.

I was already considering maybe slapping on an episode of *Coronation Street* after the good doctor when I let myself into my apartment ten minutes later, balancing my bag and the food while pulling the keys out of the lock as the door slammed shut behind me. But my musings were cut short when I reached for the light switch and nothing happened.

Dammit. Was the fuse blown? I fumbled my way

through the hallway in the darkness toward my kitchen, praying it could be fixed by flipping random switches in the fuse box. Getting an electrician out after hours in London was about as likely as seeing a rainbow-colored unicorn strutting down the street wearing a tutu.

It wasn't until I got to the kitchen that I realized I wasn't alone in the flat.

Something scraped against the floor in my living room, but even before I'd managed to convince myself it must have been something outside making a weird noise, I heard the unmistakable sound of boots against the wooden floors, making their way toward the hallway. Cutting off my only escape route.

My pulse surged as I spun around, mindlessly groping for a weapon from my kitchen counter. I grabbed a wooden handle and ripped my weapon to me, dropping the Kung Pao on the floor.

"I know you're there!" I hissed, my voice sounding somewhat more steady than I felt.

The steps stopped right in the doorway to the kitchen, and then a cone of light momentarily blinded me as someone switched on a flashlight.

I squinted against it, not wanting to lose track of my would-be assailant—and realized my weapon of choice was a wooden spoon.

"Hello, Aignéis," a cold, dreadfully familiar voice said from beyond the glare. "Or *Mira,* I suppose you go by these days."

A small whimper made its way through my throat, but I don't know how, because every single muscle in my body spasmed and then froze as the man shone the flashlight onto his own face, casting it in an eerie glow.

They had found me.

THREE
BLAINE

"You what?" I stared at my father, a bottle of beer frozen halfway on its way to my mouth.

He shot me a cold look—the one that I'd learned to take as a warning early on in my life. "I've arranged a marriage for you. It's a business deal with the Clery family from Belfast. They've been pushing for our help up north, and we unfortunately owe them. This is the best way to pay our debt without actually giving them anything of real value."

Apart from one of his sons, of course. Not that William Steel had ever seen any of us as much more than business assets.

I slammed the bottle of beer down on the kitchen counter, unable to keep my infamous temper fully in check. "Why the fuck *me*? Do I really strike you as the best husband material around?"

My father raised an eyebrow at me. "You're my oldest available son, so the task falls to you. Besides, married life might do you some good. There's no reason to kick up a fuss about this, Blaine. You're going to go to the church, you're going to marry the girl and sit through the reception so the Clerys can show off their new connection, and then you can do whatever the hell you want, as long as you make sure your wife doesn't get herself killed by any of our enemies along the way. Though it would suit you to breed a couple of heirs while you're at it—it's way past time one of you began expanding the bloodline."

I bit back a snide remark about me being the oldest *available* son. If he hadn't sent Jeremy to the U.S. to strengthen his business ties across the pond, and Isaac wasn't in jail, then I would have been third down on the list of sons to get married off to improve the *business*. Not to mention I had absolutely zero intention of "expanding the bloodline." Ever. But I knew better than to challenge him. He would send every ounce of his considerable power to back me against any of the other crime families in town. Hell, he would even back me against the police if need be, but cross him... Cross him, and it no longer mattered that we were blood.

I'd learned that much from what happened to Isaac.

I took a swig from the beer bottle, suddenly itching for something stronger. "When?"

"Next Saturday." My father got up from the barstool he'd been perched on without ever taking off his coat. Then again, it had taken him less than ten minutes from stepping through my doorway to completely and irrevocably fuck up my life, so why bother getting comfortable, right?

I gritted my teeth to stifle the black rage churning in my gut while he made his way out of my kitchen and to the front door. When his gloved hand touched the knob, he paused for a moment and looked at me over his shoulder, steel in his eyes and his jaw set in a way I recognized all too well from my youth. My hands clenched as if to brace for a beating, even though it'd been years since I'd grown too big for that particular brand of incentive.

"And Blaine... if you fuck this up, you're going to be sorry."

I stared mutely for several long minutes after he'd left, too stunned to move.

I guess it wasn't a huge surprise that it was now my turn to get dragged to the sacrificial altar for *"The Family,"* but never in a million years would I have imagined it would be as a fucking *groom.*

The thought of being tied down and responsible for a bird had always filled me with cold dread, and the fact that my upcoming marriage was a sham didn't make me feel any less shackled.

Finally, blessedly, anger drowned out the mixture of emotions coursing through me, its hot embrace allowing me to break free of the trance-like state my dear father had left me in.

Whoever the little cunt was, I wasn't about to change my ways. If she had hopes of taming herself one of Steel's sons, she was in for a nasty surprise.

I liked to drink, I liked to fight, and I liked to fuck every female that crossed my path, and if she wanted to be part of the Steel family, she was going to have to get used to that.

And maybe if I was lucky, she'd get fed up and get this fucking disaster of a marriage annulled.

I grabbed my leather coat and pulled out my phone, calling the twins as I slammed the front door shut behind me and headed down the stairs.

Time to get shitfaced and find a small-time gang dumb enough to challenge a Steel.

***

"YOU LOOK LIKE ABSOLUTE SHIT." For a man who'd kept me company during most of my weeklong bender, Liam's voice was much too cheerful. I sent him an annoyed glare, which I immediately regretted as the sunlight caught my eyes and shot a bolt of pure agony directly into my brain.

Even his unruly, ginger hair looked offensively chipper.

"You really should have thought this through," his identical twin, Louis, chimed in. "How are you going to satisfy your wee Irish lass tonight when you're so hungover you look like you're about to pass out?"

"Poor girl's in for such a disappointment—if she's desperate enough to agree to marry you, she undoubtedly needs a good rogering. Heck, she might even be a virgin! You really should bring your A-game, brother." Liam grinned.

"You two fuckers better just shut up and thank your lucky star that it's me here instead of one of you," I growled, though the twins obviously didn't share my lack of amusement. Of course, while they were standing by my side as the guests found their seats, I would be the one to swear sacred vows to a woman I'd never even met before, while they got to continue on with their lives as they pleased.

"To be fair, it would have been Marcus before either of us," Louis said, slanting a look at our only other, present brother. "For once, being the youngest of the bunch paid off."

"Ha, can you imagine them trying to marry some poor girl off to Marcus, though?" Liam snickered. "Eh, no offense, man." The last part he mumbled, the perpetual laugh in his voice dying to a cough.

I glanced at Marcus just in time to catch the dark

look he sent our way before once again looking straight ahead as if lost in deep thought.

Most sane criminals in town—and quite a few law enforcers—would make sure not to get in the way of a Steel, but Marcus had a way of making people cross the street just by looking at them. Of course, his reputation as a complete sociopath didn't help matters much.

Even I didn't really know what went on behind his blank expression, but I'd been to clean up a few of his messes along the way, and knew that he had some demons, for sure. He didn't just kill—he butchered.

"God, the Clerys are such a bunch of pricks," Louis muttered, and my attention was drawn to the front row, where a bunch of strangers filed in across the hall from our own father and stepmother. "Look at those smug smiles—they really think they hit the jackpot, eh?"

I didn't answer, but despite my blinding headache, I couldn't help but frown at the older man as he stared up at me like I was a prime cow up for auction. Undoubtedly the father, as he looked especially pleased with himself. Yeah, the Clerys obviously thought this marriage was their way up in the underworld, even if my own father saw it as nothing more than a means of placation.

My musings were interrupted when organ music abruptly blared through the church, cutting through my suffering brain like a saw. I winced and looked up just in time to see the doors at the other end of the aisle crack open.

"Here we go—time to get hitched, brother."

I didn't know which of the twins spoke, but I didn't turn my head to find out. My eyes were glued to the double doors and my heart suddenly decided to work overtime, pounding behind my ribs as if I'd just run a fucking marathon.

The doors opened fully, and a lone woman in a hideous white dress and a long veil covering her face stepped through.

I had a vague notion that it was odd her father wasn't walking her down the aisle, but my pulse thundering in my ears drowned out the thought quickly enough. Even my palms were clammy.

Fucking great. I already hated whoever she was for landing me in this fucked up situation—the fact that just seeing her walk toward me had the power to damn near bring on a panic attack didn't make me any more of a fan. I liked being in control, of myself and my surroundings, and right now, I was neither.

I didn't give a shit if it was unfair—I blamed her.

It wasn't until she was right in front of me that I realized she was looking down at the floor behind her veil, and how badly her hands were shaking as she clutched her bouquet.

A nudge to my side from Liam made me step

forward to greet her, and it was then that she finally looked up and I saw her face.

My heart gave a violent spasm before it dropped all the way to the bottom of my Italian leather shoes.

I knew her.

And her name wasn't Aignéis Clery. It was Holler. Mira Holler. My fucking shrink.

FOUR

MIRA

I'd never seen so much emotion on a completely blank face before. While every single muscle on my husband-to-be's face was still, I could practically read his mind from the flashes of shock, fear—and finally anger—that filtered across those stormcloud eyes of his. Yeah, I was about the last person he wanted to see right now.

Not that that was a surprise—the son of London's biggest crime family had gone to see a therapist, undoubtedly expecting to never be confronted with it again, only to now be forced into marrying the very same woman—possibly the only person in the world who knew that Blaine Steel had a weakness.

And I... I was beyond shocked. Not to mention annoyed at myself for not even bothering to ask who would be waiting for me at the altar. Though to be fair, I'd spent the week locked up in my own flat with no phone or computer access, effectively a prisoner. I'd been too terrified to even think about who I'd be marrying, and neither my father nor my brothers had bothered to inform me of such an unimportant detail. All that mattered to them was that they would now be related to the biggest crime family in the country.

I swallowed thickly as I stared, wide-eyed, up at Blaine. I'd run away from home the day I turned eighteen so I could escape this exact fate—so I wouldn't end up married to a man as ruthless and dangerous as the ones in my own family. Yet here I was, staring into the eyes of a man I knew without a shadow of a doubt was the living embodiment of every nightmare I'd ever had. My groom.

One of the redheaded groomsmen demonstratively cleared his throat, which made both Blaine and I jolt out of what probably looked like a staring match to the onlookers.

With one final, dark look, Blaine took my arm and turned us toward the altar, where the priest stood ready to bind us together for all eternity.

I didn't think it was possible to be any more terrified of my fate than I already was, but the look Blaine gave me held so much fury and resentment that the only thing that made me capable of following him the final few steps to the altar was the fresh wave of adrenaline coursing in my blood.

He *hated* me.

THE CEREMONY WAS A BLUR, and I have no idea how I made it through the entire thing without my anxiety making me break down into a sobbing mess. All I really comprehended through the pomp and circumstance was the sound of my own pulse drumming unsteadily in my ears.

Blaine must have led me through it, though, because when I finally snapped out of it, it was in the middle of the reception. I was seated at a table with a pretty, but untouched, dessert on my plate in a room full of laughing people I mostly didn't know or had spent years hiding from. Everyone was dressed up, there were flowers everywhere, and music underlined the chattering and laughter.

It looked like the perfect wedding, I numbly realized. Picture perfect, in fact.

If only the guest list wasn't made up of some of the worst criminals in the country and the bride hadn't been kidnapped and married off against her will.

A hysterical giggle bubbled out of my chest, only to die in a wheeze.

"You doing okay there?"

I snapped my head around to the speaker, dimly recognizing one of the redheaded groomsmen as he leaned over from a few seats away. The spaces between us were vacated, and I realized the dinner was over and most people must have left their seats for the bar, or perhaps to mingle—or whatever people did at arranged business weddings. Including my groom.

His eyes were the same color as Blaine's, but light and cheerful rather than broody and angry.

"No." The same frantic giggle escaped again, and I shook my head to make it stop. "Not even remotely. But the flowers are nice, aren't they?"

The groomsman cocked his head, his eyes turning slightly less cheerful as they roamed over my face.

"I'm getting Blaine, hang on," he said before he got up from the table and walked off toward what looked like the bar.

Great. Seeing Blaine was about the last thing I wanted, but extraordinarily poor problem-solving skills aside, at least the redhead tried. It was the first time anyone had shown any consideration for my well-being since I walked in the door to find my father in my flat, and it was enough to shake me out of the shock that had kept me shielded from the world.

It was odd, really. I had spent the entire week so terrified that my mind had shut me away from every-thing that happened around me, practically leaving me a living doll. I had gone through the motions when my mother arrived to take measurements for my wedding dress and while she and some distant cousins got me ready earlier this morning. I hadn't even objected while the people I feared most in this world took away my freedom and my choices to sell me off like a farm animal.

But when I finally snapped out of it again, in the middle of my own wedding reception, fear wasn't the emotion that rushed through my body and washed away the last tendrils of stupor.

No, it was a refreshing wave of anger.

I wasn't a bloody doll—and I damn well wasn't a trinket to be exchanged for power and influence!

"Why don't you two go up to the suite, eh? Everyone's had the chance to see the happy couple now, so you may as well spend some time getting acquainted in private."

I snapped my head in the direction of the speaker in time to see the groomsman from before waggle his ginger eyebrows at me. Behind him, Blaine stood, a glass of amber liquor in one hand and the other shoved down one pocket. Even in a tux he managed to look devil-may-care.

"Sure, may as well get started on securing the proud Steel-Clery lineage. Or should I say Steel-Holler lineage, eh, wifey?"

I got up from my seat with a glare in Blaine's direction. "You should say whatever you damn well please, because there's not going to be any lineage-making here, I can tell you that much."

He whistled and took a swig from his glass. "Your daddy's gonna be ever so disappointed."

I repressed a shudder at the reminder of my father and brushed past the two men, intent on getting out of there before I got any more reminders. The one good thing to come out of this disaster of a day was that I would never have to see him or the rest of my family ever again. The worst had already happened, and they'd have no more use for me now that they'd traded me in for better connections.

I blinked as a thought hit me while I waited in the elevator for Blaine to exchange a few words with his groomsman before he joined me, glass still in hand.

In an odd sense, I was free now. I would never again have to look over my shoulder out of fear that my family would find me. They already had, and now there was nothing more they could do to me. They had taken the life I had fought so hard for from me, but in doing so, they had given up their power over me as well. I didn't know much about Blaine, but I did know that his family was the most powerful crime syndicate in London—or else I wouldn't have been forced to marry him. Which meant that not even my father, the most brutal and ruthless man in Belfast, would have the power to ever touch me.

For better or worse, I was a Steel now.

And my family could never hurt me again.

Blaine made a sound of protest when I grabbed the glass out of his hand and downed the remaining liquor in one swig. Whiskey. It burned my throat, but I relished the fire. When it hit my—empty—stomach, a pleasant wave of euphoria mixed with my already present anger into a weirdly exhilarating combination of... of power. For the first time in a very long time, I felt strong.

No one was ever going to push me around or make me cower. Yes, the worst had happened, but I was still standing, still alive. And I was free.

"So you lie to your patients about your name. What kind of a quack are you, anyway?"

Well, sort of free. I gave Blaine an irritated look. "My name's Mira Holler, and it will always be Mira Holler."

"Well, it'll be Mira Steel from today," he said, shrugging as the elevator doors slid open and revealed the penthouse floor of the hotel we were at. I hadn't had the presence of mind to notice its name on our way here.

Blaine led the way to the only set of doors on the floor, found the key card in his tux pocket, and let us in.

I trailed after him, having nowhere else to go, and paused at the look of the suite once the door closed behind me. Everything was glass, gold, and white, with fresh flowers adorning all surfaces. Along the far wall, massive windows displayed a striking view of London and the Thames, the curtain of night interrupted by the multitude of lights from the city.

Blaine didn't give the luxurious surroundings so much as a second look. He went straight for the mini bar and filled two glasses with liquor and ice. He held one out to me while taking a long draw from his own glass.

I walked over to him and snatched the offered glass out of his hand. The burn of whiskey on my tongue was oddly comforting, and I drank deeply. Too deeply, for someone my size who up until today drank maybe once in a blue moon, but I didn't care much at that point. Getting hideously drunk seemed like a perfectly reasonable response to everything that'd happened.

"You're not going to like being married to me." Blaine leaned back against the bar and looked at me with something akin to a challenge in his stormy eyes.

I snorted. "No shit."

"It's not too late to get an annulment."

A jolt of excitement shot through me. "You'd do that?"

"Me? Fuck no." He downed the rest of his drink and poured himself another, eying me over his shoulder as he did. "If that'd been an option I'd have just said no to this whole bloody arrangement to begin with."

I stared at him, the anger making itself known again with a heated rush of blood to my cheeks and chest. "You think *I* would have gone through with this if I'd had a choice? This may come as a shock to you, *Mr. Steel*, but you're not exactly Prince Charming. I would quite literally rather marry the homeless guy who reeks of moldy cheese and asks me to suck his cock every time

I pass him on my way to work than I would you, but here we are!"

Blaine snorted, emptying half his glass of whiskey in one swig. "Here we are indeed, *Mrs. Steel.* Guess you'll just have to get used to sucking my cock instead, huh?"

I blinked. Twice. He was obviously as unhappy about this forced marriage as I was, yet he still found the energy to be a grade-A prick.

"You're a pig," I hissed. "Don't for one second think I'll put up with any of your crap just because I'm forced to live with you."

"You'll put up with exactly what I say you will." He was angry too, his eyes flashing darkly at me. "I'm your husband now, whether you like it or not, so you better get used to doing as you're told."

The same urge to slap him as I'd experienced in our disaster of a therapy session made my palms itch, but despite my—partly alcohol-fueled—bravery, I wasn't dumb enough to test my luck. Instead, I grabbed the bottle of whiskey from the bar next to him and stomped toward the white-and-gold painted door I presumed led to the bedroom.

"I'm going to bed," I announced, before I slammed the door behind me with a satisfyingly dramatic bang.

FIVE

MIRA

To my great relief, someone had filled the bedroom wardrobe with clothing, and upon closer inspection, it turned out that half of it was mine. Perhaps I should have felt violated that someone had gone through my personal belongings without my knowledge or consent to bring it here, but it seemed so insignificant compared to everything else my family had done that I was just grateful I could get out of the uncomfortable wedding dress my mother had picked out and into something soft and familiar.

When I walked into the en-suite bathroom and caught a look of myself in the mirror, I was suddenly extra glad I had my own clothes available—I looked like a big, poofy nightmare. My mother had decided on puff sleeves, a full skirt that accentuated my already rounder-than-ideal hips, and so many sequins it looked like a fairy had had an acute round of diarrhea all over me.

But it wasn't just the dress that composed the horrifying image that stared back at me from the mirror. It was also my face.

It wasn't so much the makeup—I never bothered to wear much, if any, so the lack of pizazz wasn't unusual—as it was the red rims underneath my eyes and the pale, taut look of my skin. I looked like an abuse victim—all that was lacking was a badly covered bruise or two.

Angrily, I tore off the dress, ripping it in my haste. I wasn't a victim—not anymore.

I took a swig of the bottle I'd hijacked from Blaine, and then I went to work.

There were bottles of tonics and lotions on the shelves next to the sink, and I didn't hold back. I washed and scrubbed and sprayed and smeared until my skin glowed rosy and the woman who looked back from the mirror was closer to who I'd become in the past eight years rather than who I'd been for the first eighteen of my life.

When I loosened my hair from the tight braid it had been in all day and ran my fingers through it, some of the tension in my shoulders finally melted away. My chestnut locks fell over my shoulders in unruly waves, encircling my breasts and upper arms.

I grazed a hand over the white scars on my soft belly as I looked at myself in the mirror. Not that any amount of scrubbing would ever make *those* go away. The permanent reminder of who I'd been—the unbreakable proof of my inherent weakness. I hated them almost as much as I hated the people who had put them there.

Fighting a shudder, I pulled the nightie I'd brought from the closet over my head and slipped on a pair of panties before taking a final slug of the whiskey. Dwelling on that was not what I needed right now. Blaine Steel was a dangerous man—I knew that on a near-instinctive level, but I couldn't fall back into my old patterns. I had to be strong enough to get through this, just as I'd somehow made it through the night I'd gotten my scars.

The bedroom was dark when I finally stepped out of the bathroom. I frowned into the shadows, not remembering when I'd turned the lights off, but I was a bit too drunk to give it a second thought.

Instead, I fumbled my way to the large bed I could vaguely make out in the small bit of light that made its way through the curtains, intent on falling into a deep, dreamless sleep. Tomorrow was a new day, and I was planning on spending it teaching Blaine that he wouldn't be pushing me around.

I found my way to the big bed without stubbing my toes on the wooden frame and—with a bit more fumbling—located a nightstand where I dropped off my glasses and the bottle of whiskey, and then climbed in.

The soft embrace of the mattress and duvets was

heaven. I sighed at the feel of cool sheets wrapping around my body, and again as I rolled over to bury myself good and proper in the middle of the luxurious sensation.

And that's when my hand hit something hard and warm and decidedly skin-like.

I've never shrieked quite like I did then. The mixed shock of realizing I wasn't alone in the room—or even the bed—and the unexpectedness at touching someone made me lift at least half a foot off the sheets.

"What the actual fuck!" I rolled to the bedside table and searched wildly for a lamp until my fingers finally connected with a button and I illuminated the room.

Blaine—topless Blaine—squinted at me from the other side of the bed. "Fuck, you could deafen dogs with that scream."

I stared at him, mouth halfway open, as my addled brain tried to process the situation. Which unfortunately included the full view of Blaine's ridiculously chiseled, tattoo-covered torso. I couldn't stop my eyes from following the pattern of swirling lines until he cleared his throat demonstratively, and I realized I'd been ogling him for a good thirty seconds at least.

"Changed your mind about that shag, then?"

It was impressive, really. He had a gift for sounding equal parts annoyed and smug, and the result was absolutely infuriating.

"Get out of my bed!" I was all too aware of the heat

in my cheeks, but I did my best to push the embarrassment aside and focus on the indignity of finding him near-naked in bed with me. I pulled the duvet up to cover my chest, but regretted it the next second. Apparently, he wasn't just near-naked.

"Jesus Christ!" I clamped my mouth shut, but not before my startled exclamation made it impossible to pretend like I hadn't seen anything.

As if it wasn't bad enough that I was now staring at his cock. No, it was made so much worse—and it was freaking enormous. And semi-erect.

Blaine stretched out, folding his arms behind his head. He was obviously enjoying my flustered state. "I'm not going anywhere. This is my bed too, if you remember—wifey."

"You're not going to sleep next to me, you creep!" I hissed, doing my best not to look below his navel again. The problem was that restriction either left me with his hard abs and chiseled pecs, or his smirking face. With as much dignity as I could muster I turned around so I could no longer see him at all. "There's a perfectly good couch in the lounge."

"Sorry love, I'm gonna be way too hungover tomorrow to wake up on a couch. You're just gonna have to deal with it." He yawned and stretched in what I was certain was the most provocative way possible, making every defined muscle in his body roll. "Turn off the light, will ya?"

"No! Get out!"

"Not a chance. But no one's stopping *you* from sleeping on the couch, are they?"

There was just enough challenge in his rumbly voice to make me see red. Perhaps in hindsight, I should have just given in and slept on the damn couch, but his arrogance—and possibly the vast amounts of whiskey—got to me. And it got to me good.

"You'd like that, wouldn't you? I'm telling you right now, you're not going to boss me around in this marriage, you absolute... twat!" I gave him a baleful glare, which I immediately regretted when my eyes caught sight of his absurdly huge cock again. Either I was hindered by my lack of glasses, or the damn thing was even bigger now than it'd been before. My cheeks flushed with heat, and I quickly tore my gaze away and flopped down on my back, arms folded over my chest. "I'm staying here—and *you* need to leave."

"Whatever you say, love."

The bed creaked, and for a moment I thought he was actually getting out. My rush of victory proved short-lived. Before I could blink, Blaine rolled over on top of me, only barely keeping off of me by resting on one arm a mere inch above the duvet. The other arm he extended out so he could turn off the lights.

I got a full view of his strong body as he hovered over me before the lights went out—just long enough for the more carnal parts of my brain to awaken.

Heat spread from low in my abdomen, racing all the way up through my body and down my thighs until I could feel my pulse throb everywhere he would touch if he lowered himself that small inch to press down on top of me.

Looking back, my body's mutinous reaction wasn't all too surprising. As much as I hated him for who he was, Blaine was so perfectly male and ruthlessly handsome most women would find it hard to breathe with him up close and personal like this—especially when he didn't have a shred of clothing on. The fact that he was as dangerous as they come seemed to have been erased by my drunken state, and the result was perfectly predictable.

Unfortunately for me, I wasn't at all prepared when my abdomen seemed to melt, the liquid proof moistening my panties in a warm rush.

My first instinct was shocked humiliation that a man I hated could make me soak my panties just by being on top of me. Then, thankfully, came the fury.

"What the *hell* do you think you're doing?" I slapped my hands up, both palms connecting with his pecs with a satisfying *smack*. "Get off me!"

Above me in the darkness, Blaine hissed at the impact. "Don't *ever* hit me again." It was a warning.

Perhaps if I'd been sober, I would have taken his threat to heart, even through my own fury. Too bad I was anything but.

"Or what, you'll beat me bloody? Slit my throat? Exactly how much violence do you need to inflict to feel like a tough guy?" I shoved his shoulders in an attempt to get him off me, but all that accomplished was to make him lose his balance so he fell down on top of the duvet, pinning my body to the mattress with his.

"I'd never harm a woman—even if she is the most obnoxious little bitch I've ever met." Blaine raised up on both arms this time, and I could sense him hovering above me as close as before. "But if you push me again, you're going to be sorry."

I pushed him. Hard. Because fuck him—and the horse he rode in on. "I'm not afraid of you!"

He moved above me, quick as a snake, and I scrambled to get out from underneath him. Sadly for me, he was much faster—and stronger—and before I'd gotten more than a leg out from underneath the duvet, he'd pinned both my wrists above my head with one hand. The other he pressed firmly against my chest, just below my throat. Not hard enough to make me struggle to breathe, but certainly so firmly I couldn't move my upper body.

"You should be." His voice was rough, and to my great annoyance, something in its pitch spoke to my core —the part of me that was whispering excitedly about being pinned underneath him. It only angered me all the more.

I kicked out with my free leg and got it hooked

around the back of his hamstrings, digging my heel into the back of his knee as hard as I could muster. "Get off!"

"Ow!" Blaine flinched and pulled back, which gave me enough momentum to rip my wrists out of his hands and twist around to my stomach in an attempt at getting out from underneath him.

"You little tramp!" Just as I clawed my way halfway to the other side of the wide bed, large hands grabbed my shoulders, and Blaine clamped his knees around my thighs tight, stopping me mid-flight. I kicked out again and caught something solid with the flat of my foot.

Blaine grunted, undoubtedly from pain. "Fine, if you want it like that..." He slid his hands down my sides along my nightie from my shoulders to my hips, pausing only for a second before he grabbed my hips and pulled me up on my knees so my arse was in the air, my face still pressed against the mattress.

He wouldn't...! I gasped in scandalized protest as a sense of foreboding set in, but it was too late.

Blaine let go of my hip with one hand, and in the next moment, he brought his palm down against my upturned backside. But when it connected with my panty-clad flesh, it wasn't pain that made me gasp out. The light must have made him misjudge his target, and when he spanked me, his hand slapped fully against the puffy lips of my sex rather than my arse.

He had obviously planned on proving who was boss rather than cause me any pain when he swung, because if it had landed on my fleshy backside, it wouldn't even have really stung. But, as I realized while I lay there in shocked silence, there's quite a bit of a difference between your arse and your private parts, and the feel of his hand still seemed to vibrate through my now molten flesh. Every inch of my skin down there was alive with sensation, and I could feel my clit throbbing hard between my lower lips.

I'd never been so turned on in my entire life.

"You're dripping wet." The hoarse note was back in his voice, even more pronounced now.

Oh *fuck*. Of course he would have noticed that.

Only my still-present anger kept complete mortification at bay.

Angrily, I pulled free from his grasp and turned around so I could glare in his direction.

"I am not! I swear to God, don't even think about touching me again!"

"Or what? You'll beg me to fuck you?" Whatever anger had been in Blaine's voice before, it was gone now —overtaken by that smug self-assuredness I'd come to loathe already, along with something else. Something quite a bit more appealing, if my ovaries were to be believed. It made the heat from my sex spread up through my stomach and underneath my skin.

"You're such a prick!" I hissed, but even to my own ears, I sounded more breathy than I did angry. Which was bullshit—I *was* angry! Blaine shifted on the bed and

I kicked out, hitting him square in the stomach. But before I could retract my foot, Blaine grabbed me by the ankle and pulled, sending me flat on my back with an undignified huff.

"Let go you arsehole!"

"Seems like you're the one who can't stop touching me." He pulled on my ankle again, making me slide further down toward him, and then he put his other hand on my free leg, effectively keeping me from kicking out again.

"I'm not *touching* you, you goon," I growled. "I'm trying to get away from you."

"Sure you are, love." He shifted again, letting his hands slide along my legs to keep me in place as he moved up my body. There was no duvet between us this time, and I felt his warm skin against mine like a touch of maddening fire as his hands made their way to my hips. "I'm sure you'll be dry as a desert if I slip my fingers into your knickers as well, hmm?"

His cockiness was so goddamn infuriating! I kicked out again, but this time he was prepared. I didn't so much as graze him, and before I could roll away, he grabbed ahold of my hips and tugged hard—and then proceeded to push his hard body down on top of mine.

I froze at the press of his muscular frame. From the feel of his heavy mass pinning me to the warmth of his skin and the smell of whiskey on his breath, his closeness enveloped me—and whatever damned hormones had control over my body went wild. My nipples tightened until they ached, and a veritable flood of liquid made my already soaking panties even wetter.

"Let's test, shall we?" He murmured into my ear. His hot breath tickled my skin and made me break out into goosebumps. "If you're dry, I'll go sleep on the couch. If you're wet... we fuck."

SIX

MIRA

"I don't want to sleep with you." I was pretty proud of the sneer in my voice, despite how the word "fuck" whispered into my ear in his molten voice nearly made my ovaries explode. "Keep your hands to yourself!"

"No dice." Blaine shifted his hold on me so he could keep both my wrists in one hand, spread my legs with his knees—and then proceeded to reach down, his fingertips grazing against the front of my panties.

The thin fabric clung to my skin from the wetness, and when he trailed his fingers further down, I knew he could feel the outline of my lips without any problems.

I shuddered at the trickle of desire that followed, but bit back a wanton moan out of spite. I'd be damned if I'd give him the satisfaction of knowing how strongly I reacted to him—even if it was impossible to hide the ruined state of my panties.

Then he slipped his fingers underneath the fabric and brushed up and down my slit a few times before caressing my taut clit.

I couldn't hold back a sharp gasp as a burst of pleasure rocked through me, nor could I stop my legs from widening further, pushing my pelvis up in an involuntary invitation.

"Soaked." Blaine removed his hand from my panties and held it up between us. I couldn't see much, but the scent of my arousal was heavy in the air between us. He breathed in deeply and then sucked on his fingers with a lewd pop. "And fucking delicious."

"You're an evil prick." Despite the harsh words, my voice lacked any sort of conviction. The fog of lust made it impossible to remember why I hated him so much.

"You're an obnoxious prude." Blaine's snarl had all the richness of a prowling tiger. He tugged on my panties again, once to test and then once more, hard, snapping the waistband with ease. "And you're gonna get fucked."

I gasped when he touched my pussy again, fully this time. He rubbed along my puffy lips, coating his thumb before he pressed in hard against my clit.

"Blaine!" I was only half aware that I'd cried out his name when he began circling the little nub, too overcome with the sharp sensations of pure bliss that rocked through my nerves for every round of his thumb.

It felt like nothing had before. Maybe it was the

week's worth of tension finally finding a way to be released, or perhaps it was just the sheer animal attraction I'd had for him ever since he walked into my office. Whatever it was, it left me blind-sided, panting and whimpering for his touch like a cat in heat.

"Inside! I need you inside!" I arched my back up, desperate to feel what my body craved with every pulse of blood through my veins. It didn't matter that he was a cocky bastard, nor that I was faintly aware that I was meant to be scared of him. All that mattered was his hard body and the thickness I'd glimpsed between his legs earlier. He had what I needed, and I needed it now. I dug my nails into his chest to make sure he understood my urgency.

Blaine grunted as my nails penetrated his skin, but it worked as intended. He shifted above me, and suddenly his fingers were replaced by something warm, hard, and *thick.*

"*Fuck!*" His hissed outburst drowned out the hitch in my breath when he pressed in, seating the head of his fat cock with one push. "Damn, you're tight."

I whimpered in response. It had been so long since I'd been with a man, and Blaine wasn't just equipped for show. My channel trembled around him, fighting to accommodate his girth, but all I felt was pure, unadulterated desire. I needed him deep, and I needed him *now.*

"More! Give me more!"

"And so goddamn demanding," he added, but he obeyed nevertheless. A flex of his hips and his thick cock drove home, all the way to my very core.

"*Oh!*" I dug my nails into him again, too overcome with the sensation of being filled to the brim to care if I drew blood. This was exactly what I needed—to be taken, to fuck—to lose my mind to the sweet rush of endorphins. "God, yes!"

Blaine didn't give me much of a chance to get used to the feel of being penetrated so deeply. With a grunt he pulled his hips back, only to slam them against mine again the next second. I cried out as wild pleasure ripped through my pelvis and wrapped my legs around his hamstrings, mindlessly clutching on to the source of the ecstasy.

Again he moved, and I moved with him, rolling my hips up to meet his blows, even as the power of them made a dull ache mix with the pleasure. It didn't matter —I wanted it hard, and I needed it rough. I bit his shoulder and scratched his back to make him give me everything he had.

An animalistic snarl ripped from Blaine's throat, and the next second, I learned exactly what it meant to be truly and thoroughly *fucked*.

He grabbed my hands and pinned them above my head. And then he unleashed every ounce of that barely-contained fury I'd seen in his eyes all day.

Blaine's thick cock pounded into me, forcing my

pussy wide all the way to the depths of my being. The thick rim of his head rubbed the full length of my tight sheath, pummeling my G-spot over and over and over. His hips slapped against my arse, beating the brutal rhythm into my flesh as well as my pussy. He moved like a demon possessed, forcing me to take every inch with no mercy and no respite.

It was exactly what I needed.

The dull ache in me turned to pain at his roughness, but I relished it all the more. And underneath him, I finally let go.

I screamed until my throat was sore, I thrashed and bucked and cried. All the fear, all the anger and despair —I released it all while the man who was now my husband despite both our wishes fucked me like I'd never even imagined possible.

When I finally crested, he came with me.

Pleasure so strong it felt like it would splinter my pelvis ripped through my abdomen from my pussy and spread into every cell of my body, leaving me numb and completely unable to move. I was faintly aware of Blaine's gasp of pleasure and the warm rush of his semen deep inside, but not even when he kissed my jawline a few times before brushing his mouth against mine did I manage to wrestle my mind free of its endorphin high. Everything was calmness and bliss, and for the first time in as long as I could remember, I was truly at peace.

SEVEN

BLAINE

Ow. Fucking hell, ow!

I groaned in protest of the sharp pain piercing my skull from the inside the moment I crackedked open my eyes.

Even the faint light that filtered in through the curtains was too bright, and I quickly shut them again. Judging by the taste in my mouth, I'd overdone it on the whiskey. By a lot.

A jumbled mess of images stumbled through my brain, as if to helpfully remind me of every single glass I'd downed. I frowned when a fuzzy memory of Liam attempting to stop me from ordering another glass at the bar surfaced. How very uncharacteristic.

He'd said something about... my wife needing me.

The shock of realization when the rest of yesterday's

horrors came crashing back to my recollection made me open my eyes wide—a move I instantly regretted.

"Fuck." I hurriedly squeezed them shut once more, but only after the light of day had penetrated into what felt like the stem of my suffering brain.

I had a *wife*.

Slowly, I became aware of the heavy press of a warm body against mine.

Oh. Right. We fucked, didn't we?

Despite my pain, I couldn't hold back a lazy smile over that particular part of last night's events. Turned out the little prude was quite the wildcat after all. If memory served, I was pretty sure I'd be sporting some scratches today.

Carefully I cracked my eyelids again, bracing for the pain this time. It took a while, but once my eyes had adjusted, I could see without wanting to dig out my own brain with a spoon.

She was laying halfway on my shoulder, with one leg and an arm thrown across my body and her chestnut hair spread around her head like a sheet of darkened blood. She was also drooling.

Mira. Or Aignéis, or whatever the fuck she was called.

I hadn't noticed an Irish accent on her when I'd seen her the first time, nor last night, even though it was thick in both her father and two brothers. I hadn't heard her mother speak, but assumed it was the same. The Clerys were Irish through and through—yet apart from the pale skin and auburn hair, my new wife showed no sign of her heritage.

Wife. Fuck.

I'd planned to pretty much ignore the girl unlucky enough to be chosen for my bride, but seeing *her* standing there in that damned church floored me.

If I'd known there was even the smallest chance I'd ever run into her again, I would never in a million years have gone to a psychologist—no matter how desperate I was. And I'd been pretty fucking desperate.

I sighed, making Mira's long hair move and tickle against my arm on the blow out. If anyone ever knew I'd been so weak I'd sought out help from a bloody shrink, I was done for. There was no room for weakness in this world, nor anyone who couldn't cope with the dark parts of the job. And yet I'd cracked. I'd given in to the demons in my head and showed my soft underbelly—showed it to *her*.

Which made her more dangerous than any of my family's multitude of enemies.

I stared down at her face. She looked innocent in her sleep. Vulnerable, even. Completely at odds with the copious amounts of attitude I'd seen from her so far.

She *hated* me, probably even more so than I hated her part in this arrangement, but as she lay by my side, it was hard to remember that she was a threat.

I probably shouldn't have shagged her, but I'd

wanted to from the first time I laid eyes on her round arse when I first walked into her office. Still did, if my stiff cock was to be believed. Which it was.

I reached over and let my hand slide down her shoulder to her soft chemise. It was a flattering violet color, but I was more interested in the way it hugged her ample cleavage when she lay on her side. I traced a thumb across one breast and smirked when her nipple perked under my caress. Seemed her body was as fond of me as mine was of her.

She didn't look like the usual type of girl I fucked. I tended to gravitate toward tall, slender model types, mainly because they were the ones who hung around the clubs I went to.

Mira was short and deliciously full-figured, and my cock had ached to be buried between her generous thighs from first sight. All the sex I'd had before seemed so plain and dull in comparison, like rice crackers next to a feast of abundance. And once I was finally inside of her...

My cock throbbed eagerly at the memory. Who knew a rough hate-fuck would end up the best sex of my damned life?

I drew a teasing circle around her tight nipple and saw the small bud harden into a full peak.

Should have taken the time to explore her luscious little body some more, but the desperate need to be inside of her hadn't left time for such luxuries.

I glanced at Mira's sleeping face. Maybe she'd be up for seconds. Nothing beat lazy morning sex as a hangover cure, and we could always go back to hating each other after an orgasm or two. Or three.

I slipped my hand down her side and up underneath her chemise, eager to feel more of her warm skin. When I brushed across her soft stomach, something slightly rough and raised on her skin made me pause. It felt like scar tissue. My fingertips danced across it for a few moments, but the small burst of curiosity at the unexpected appearance of scars on her abdomen was quickly smothered by my cock's desperate pulsing. Demanding fucker.

I pushed further up until my questing hand reached her soft breast. It felt even better without fabric covering it. I squeezed the plump flesh gently.

Mira murmured sleepily in response, and I quirked my head to see if she was waking up.

Her eyes were still firmly shut, and her face relaxed. No such luck.

Hmm.

Carefully, I rolled her off my shoulder—wiping her drool off my skin with a grimace—so I could maneuver better. She grumbled in obvious protest at the loss of contact, but still didn't wake.

Mira was a heavy sleeper, apparently. At least after half a bottle of whiskey.

I dragged the loose neckline of her cleavage down

far enough to let both breasts spill over the edge of the fabric, and hummed appreciatively at the sight before latching one to one of the peachy pink little nubs.

Mira mumbled in her sleep again. It sounded more like a moan this time, and it made an aching spasm travel down the length of my cock. Yeah, morning sex was so on.

I leaned over so I could rest on one elbow, letting my other hand travel down her body until it got to the heat between her thighs. I stroked one finger through her cleft while pulling gently at her nipple, and was rewarded when she spread her thighs with a sleepy sigh.

Damn, I needed to fuck her again. So much for exploring her body more carefully—one tit fondle and I was desperate to get inside her wet little snatch. What the hell kind of heroin did she hide in there?

I let my fingers find her clit, stroking it gently until she started to squirm, her breathing no longer deep and peaceful. Then I delved a finger inside of silken folds and was rewarded with the drenched embrace of her cunt.

She soaked so easily for me, it was a wonder she'd managed to put up so much of a fight before finally caving. I smirked at the knowledge that the prim and proper psychologist who had thrown me out of her office for asking for a fuck was as attracted to my body as any other red-blooded female I'd come across since hitting puberty. Perhaps even more so, if her pussy's slick welcome was any indicator.

I slipped another finger into her while keeping my thumb busy on her clit, and this time, her response was a full-throated moan. Seemed like she was coming to. I pumped her slowly, aching to bury my tongue between her thighs, but ego made me hold back. I wanted to see her face fall apart when I sucked on her clit, and she'd have to be fully awake for that to happen. Maybe after the first round.

I curved both fingers in her tight heat just so, hitting the spongy flesh nestled behind her pelvic bone firmly.

"Blaine."

I popped my mouth off her nipple to look at her at the breathy sound of my name, but her eyes were still closed even though a frown marred her face. I rubbed against her G-spot while watching her, and nearly came at the fine tremor playing across her pretty features as she breathed shakily. Slowly, her body began to move under mine, the rhythm of my hand transferring to her hips as I brought her closer and closer.

Nope, couldn't keep watching her face or I'd end up fucking her before she woke up fully. My cock was hurting from the need to be inside of her, and watching her slowly come undone made it unbearable. Instead, I busied my mouth at her breasts again, licking and sucking at her pert nipples in time with my fingers' thrusting.

Her moans and whimpers spurred me on until her pussy clamped up tight, squeezing my fingers to a halt for two long seconds before erupting in a series of fluttering spasms. Her body seized underneath mine, and she gasped her pleasure out as I lifted my head just in time to see her eyes pop open.

"What *the fuck* are you doing?"

I gotta be honest, that wasn't exactly the response I'd expected. Nevertheless, I gave her flustered and panting face a smirk and thrilled my fingers over her undoubtedly hypersensitive G-spot. "Getting you off."

Mira jerked underneath me and grabbed at my wrist to still my teasing movements. "Get off me!"

"I would rather get off *in* yo—*uff!*" I hadn't been observant enough, and paid for my cheek when she dug a knee into my gut and pushed.

For a relatively small bird, she had a lot of leg power.

I rolled off her, pressing a hand to my now pretty sore abs, and narrowly avoided getting kicked in the dick by her flailing legs as she scrambled up to the headboard of the bed, duvet wrapped around her like a virgin hiding from some tentacled hentai beast. Her hazel eyes were large and unfocused, but the anger in them was unmistakable.

Great. Seemed like we were gonna go right back to hating each other before I'd gotten as much as a thank-you wank. I rubbed at my sore stomach and gave her an irritated glare. "What the hell was that for?"

"*What was that for...?*" Despite her obvious trouble with seeing me clearly without her glasses, she managed to look both astonished and absolutely furious at the same time. I might have been impressed, if my flagging cock didn't mean I now had enough blood left in my brain to properly feel my hangover again.

"That was for *molesting* me, you absolute twat!" Apparently, she'd had enough of not being able to focus all that anger at my face, because she reached out for her glasses on the nightstand, and managed to knock over the near-empty bottle of whiskey she'd placed there the night before in her efforts.

"Molesting you? You just came all over my hand! While moaning my name, I might add. Jesus fucking Christ, what about a 'thank-you' instead of kneeing me in the gut?"

"A '*thank-you*'?" Her voice turned shrill, and I winced as it went right through my brain. She leveled a glare at me through the black-rimmed glasses that could have turned a more easily intimidated man into stone. "Right! Then *thank you* for taking advantage at me while I was drunk and emotionally fucked up after the worst week of my life. Which, I might add, is a pretty goddamn bad week. And while I'm at it, thank you so much for marrying me against my will and ruining my life! Now kindly get the fuck out of my bed!"

Awesome. We were back to this, then.

Something that seemed an awful lot like disappointment nestled in the pit of my belly. I had no idea why—perhaps the first-class fuck had given drunk-me some half-baked hope that this arrangement wouldn't be so bad after all.

Drunk-me was a moron.

Letting the bizarre sense of disappointment be washed away by my general annoyance—at her, at my father and most definitely at my once again hard and hopeful cock—I got out of bed and stretched, rolling my shoulders to ease some of the irritation out of my body.

"Fine. If this is how you want it, this is how you'll get it." I shot her a dark look over my shoulder, letting her know exactly who she was dealing with. She might know I had a weakness, and her body might draw me in like a moth to a flame, but I was still Blaine Steel. And like it or not, she was going to have to deal with being my wife. My unwanted wife.

"Get dressed and pack your things. I'll send one of my men up to get you after exactly forty-five minutes. He will help you get your stuff down to the lobby. *Do not be late.* If I have to come get you myself, you're going to be sorry. We'll discuss the rest of the rules you'll have to live by once we're home."

Satisfied with her dumbstruck expression, I bent to snatch my clothes up from the floor and left the bedroom with as much of a door-slam as my head could handle.

If she insisted on making life hard, then I could certainly play that game too. No one bested a Steel, and the sooner the obnoxious little shrink learned that lesson, the better.

Don't leave the house without an escort
Don't go into the shed
Don't invite anyone over
Don't ask questions about visitors
Don't speak to visitors unless spoken to
Don't open the door without permission
Stop sulking

I glared at Blaine from behind the kitchen counter, where I'd been watching him write down the "house rules" in big, black letters on the fridge. My ire had grown for every line, but the final one pushed me over the edge, my irritation finally overwhelming whatever fear was left from the drive here. Being surrounded by goons was such a sharp reminder of exactly what sort of family I'd gotten married into, and Blaine had been quiet and broody ever since our confrontation in the morning. On top of how the morning had started out, I'd been too shaken to feel anything but the return of my anxiety.

That is, until the arsehole started making *The List*.

"Maybe I'd stop '*sulking*' if you stopped acting like I'm your prisoner. What's number eight going to be? That I have to ask before going to the bathroom?"

Blaine rubbed at his neck as if he was trying to work out a particularly bothersome knot, but he didn't turn around to look at me. In fact, he hadn't looked at me all day, since he left our bedroom in a huff. "I don't give a fuck about what you do when we're alone, as long as you do it inside the house. These rules are as much for your sake as they are mine."

"Go on. I can't wait to hear how it's for my own sake that I can't have visitors." I was pretty pleased with my dry tone.

He finally turned around then, and looked at me with one eyebrow cocked. "It's been a while since you've lived in this world, hasn't it?"

"You mean, since I've had to live among criminals? Yeah, it has."

Blaine capped the black marker he'd been using to write on the American-style fridge, crossed both arms over his chest so his muscles bulged against the strain of his T-shirt, and leaned a shoulder against the appliance. "My family has a lot of enemies, and you're a soft and squishy target. I can guarantee you that every single one of those enemies is trying to find a way to get to you as we speak. So say you invite a friend over, and someone watched them walk in the door here. You think many of the men who are out to get me would hesitate to snatch them off the street to find out anything they might know about us?"

I paled at that implication. No, I knew that sort of men all too well. They wouldn't hesitate to use torture if they thought they could gain an advantage.

"Want to order a pizza? If it's not checked by one of our guys, you have no guarantee it's not delivered by a hitman in disguise. Feel like taking a wander around the neighborhood? Those same men who would snatch up your friends in a second would do much, much worse to you. So you might think of yourself as a prisoner if that floats your boat, but I'm sure you'll agree it's a lot better than the alternative."

I bit my lip at his challenging stare, more than a little annoyed at his excellent use of logic. I wasn't in the mood to back down. "And the shed? What horrors will befall me if I dare venture into the backyard? You keeping a magical rose in a glass jar or something?"

Blaine grunted and shoved off the fridge so he could make his way toward the French doors between the kitchen and the hallway. "You say you've not been involved in this world for a while. Let's keep it that way."

I stared after him as he sauntered out of the room, but quickly averted my gaze when he grabbed the hem of his T-shirt and pulled it over his head, revealing his tattooed and perfectly muscled back. There was absolutely no need to see anymore of Blaine naked. Not after what had happened in that blasted hotel room.

"I'm grabbing a shower. My room's the big one on the first floor. Pick any of the others for yourself, and do whatever the fuck you want to the rest of the house," he called as he disappeared around the corner. The sound of his steps made it obvious that he was headed up the large staircase I'd seen when we came in through the front door.

Great. I looked around the large kitchen while pointedly ignoring the offensive list on the fridge. The house seemed about as warm and inviting as my new husband—no decorative touches lit up the bare surfaces and stainless steel appliances.

Not that I really wanted Blaine to be *"warm and inviting,"* no siree. My cheeks flushed hotly at the memories I'd been doing my best to suppress all day. Thanks to the hefty amounts of alcohol in my system, I didn't have a fully intact recollection of what exactly had happened between us, but my brain didn't spare me many details from the actual sex. The hot, sweaty, and ridiculously good sex.

Not that I'd been able to live in ignorance, even if my brain wasn't such a dick. Every muscle in my body hurt, like I'd been worked over good and thorough, leaving a lazy sort of ache not only in my limbs but also in the kind of places whiskey just didn't get you sore.

It had taken all I had not to limp in front of Blaine or his "men." It was bad enough I'd had the biggest lapse in judgment of all time—I wasn't about to boost the jerk's ego any further by acknowledging how stupidly well-endowed he was.

Not that he didn't already know. Logging around a cock the size of a damn water bottle was not something a man as arrogant as Blaine would be ignorant about.

God *dammit*! And here I was, obsessing about the damn thing when I should be busy either having a nervous breakdown or figuring out a plan as to how to get out of this nightmare of an arranged marriage. Just great!

I spent most of the afternoon exploring my new home, partly to keep my mind off any further unsavory thoughts of Blaine.

I had thought this was Blaine's house, but when I walked around, I saw that every room was only sparsely decorated with the necessities, and a few of them had unopened moving boxes scattered around. Seemed like we were both new occupants.

The house itself turned out to be gorgeous and absolutely huge. It was an Edwardian-style townhouse located off a quiet street, but during my initial explorations I counted six bedrooms, five living rooms, a library, and a couple of smaller, empty rooms that would likely make good offices or playrooms. I didn't count that many bathrooms, but most of the bedrooms seemed to be en-suite.

Crime had to be paying more than well for the Steels, because this house would have been so expensive it could have fed an African village for a decade.

I picked one of the smaller bedrooms located on the top floor. It wasn't the grandest of spaces, but it was plenty big enough for me, and it had a window bench with a great view over the lush back yard. Whoever had lived here before, they'd hired a superb landscaper.

After dragging my suitcase upstairs, I collapsed on the already made bed for a power nap, too physically and emotionally drained to even get undressed.

WHEN I WOKE up again it was dark outside, and my hangover seemed more or less on the retreat.

I lay in the darkness for a bit and let my mind settle in for the first time since my family found me.

And as I did, I felt myself finally start to relax a bit. Yes, the worst had happened, but I was still alive. They hadn't killed me, and as I'd realized last night in my drunken stupor, my new marriage meant that I was free of them. I might have been dragged back into the criminal underworld, but I wasn't a teenager anymore. And, dangerous as he might be, Blaine didn't seem like he would physically harm me. In fact, I'd kicked at him and he hadn't raised his hand in retaliation. Not really, anyway.

I flushed at the hazy memory of his hand smacking down between my legs. I probably should be outraged, now that alcohol wasn't fogging over my brain, but all I could muster was embarrassment—and a hot stab of desire.

No, the only physical danger I was in from Blaine was my own body's mutiny every time he got near me. Pure, carnal attraction I should be able to ignore.

Which meant it was time to face my fears and realize that I wasn't helpless anymore. I had been for the last week, locked up like a sacrificial lamb, but that was over now.

I hugged myself close and breathed deeply, repeating that phrase in my head again and again until an inkling of belief took root in my mind.

I was a grown woman now, not an abused child, and I had years of training in dealing with the human psyche. If I could help my patients, then I could help myself.

I can't say that calmness took over me as I lay there, but more a certain sense of determination that allowed me to focus like I hadn't been able to since my family found me. If I wanted out of this, then I could find my way with calm planning.

Blaine would no doubt stop me from leaving. Now that we were legally married, it would be an insult to his honor if his wife up and abandoned him. His reputation would suffer, and I knew all too well that honor was everything to men like him.

I briefly touched a hand to my midsection on top of my shirt. I couldn't feel the scars through the fabric, but I knew they were there. Ugly reminders of just how important honor was to men in this business.

But would he chase me down if I got away? I highly doubted it. Once I was out of London, the damage would have already been done, and I was under no illusion that he would grieve my departure. He and his family would be in their full right to cancel any business arrangements they'd made with my father, and likely also demand compensation, so as long as I figured out a way out of the city, Blaine wouldn't be a problem.

But my own family would.

Just the thought of my father's anger made me clench my hands in the blankets to stop them from shaking. If they found me after I'd cost them money and reputation, they would kill me. End of story.

When I ran away the first time, I'd been nothing more than a useless daughter, and I was pretty sure no one had spent much time looking for me. I'd like to think that maybe my mother had at least called around to my classmates, but who knew? It was always about the business, and I'd... I'd not been of any help there.

I bit down on my quivering lip until I tasted blood, reducing those memories to nothing more than a dark space in my consciousness. My gut twisted and I focused on breathing deeply again until the bout of anxiety passed.

Sure, talking about past trauma is good for the soul—no one knows that better than a psychologist. But I'd always known, with every bone in my body, that once I punctured that abscess, what would come pouring out would be dark and hideous. Right now, I needed to focus on forming and executing a plan to get out of my forced marriage—not digging in painful memories.

If I wanted to avoid my family, then I'd need to get further away than their network could reach, which would mean getting out of Great Britain. Getting a visa would be hard without Blaine noticing, but with the right to free travel within Europe, that didn't have to be a problem.

Which just left me with the issue of getting out of London and away from the Steels.

Right now, Blaine had zero reason to trust me, which the set of rules on the fridge so clearly displayed. He would undoubtedly have some measures ready to keep me in the house, and I had no way of knowing what or where they were—apart from the two goons who had followed us from the hotel, and who I'd seen take up a stance on each side of our front door. As effi-cient at keeping enemies out as they were at keeping me in.

But if Blaine maybe trusted me, at least a little...

My heart thumped uneasily and I pressed a hand to my chest and frowned. Scary as the thought was, perhaps getting closer to my new husband wasn't the worst of ideas.

So far, the way I'd acted around him had been more resemblant of a teenager than a grown woman. A horny teenager.

Sure, I hadn't exactly been in the best state of mind, but if I wanted him to trust me enough to afford me some slack on the rules, I'd likely need him to respect me. Yelling at him and blaming him for everything that had gone wrong was not going to get me far.

So that was it—I had a plan, even if it was still a bit rough around the edges. And the first step was to gain Blaine's respect. Get closer to him.

Might have been a lot easier if he wasn't such a dick.

NINE

BLAINE

"I'm hungry."

The sound of Mira's voice ripped me out of my brooding with a start I barely managed to camouflage with a flex of my shoulders and arms. Seemed the bird was pretty stealthy. And clearly not used to knocking.

I rolled over on my bed to face the door, where my new wife was standing, both arms wrapped around her midsection. I cocked an eyebrow at her. Not that I'd studied the subject in depth at any point, but it seemed like feeding her wouldn't fall under my husbandly duties.

"...And there's nothing in the fridge but beer and hot sauce. I'd order a pizza, but who knows if it'll come with a complimentary hit man? Or poisonous mushrooms?"

Oh. Right. Girl had a point, even if her sarcastic tone made her feelings on the rules I'd laid out for her clear. At least she wasn't shouting. "I'll order us something. And I'll get Rob to help you with planning out the household shopping tomorrow."

Her hazel eyes narrowed a bit behind her glasses. "Who's Rob?"

"My righthand man. He's in charge of security. You'll have to go through him when you set up everything you need to run the house. You can order deliveries from the supermarkets, but you'll have to make sure you only order from places where we have someone working. Rob will be able to tell you more. If you need help with cleaning and all that, he should be able to get you in contact with the woman who cleans for my father. Anything you can't buy online you'll need to arrange for one of the guys to go get." Would you look at that—Blaine Steel discussing household crap like a responsible adult. I briefly wondered if this what what my father had had in mind when he said married life would do me good.

"I'm sorry... you seem to be under the illusion that *I* will be taking care of the household?"

There was something in Mira's voice that made me hesitate for just a second. Her tone had shifted from pure sarcasm to holding some sort of warning. Then I frowned and shook it off. If she wasn't happy, it wasn't my problem.

"Yeah. What else would you do? Paint your toenails?"

She blinked. Twice. "My job. You may recall I have one of those."

Was she really that naïve, or was she just baiting me? "You don't anymore. It'd be too dangerous, and we don't have the manpower to have someone follow you around all day."

From the look on her face, she really had been that naive. A pained look of shock crossed her pretty features, and her hands fisted by her sides as her arms fell from their protective pose crossed over her midsection.

"You can't do that."

I frowned as the light from my bedside lamp caught the fresh shine in her eyes. Were those... tears? Based on our previous interactions, I'd been unsurprised at anger and shouting, but *tears?*

"I'm sorry, it's not up for negotiation." The weird thing was that, as I looked at her standing there in my doorway so shocked and upset, I *was* actually sorry. Sorry that those tears were there because of me. Which was mildly ironic, for a man who spread pain and misery for a living.

Then her expression darkened and her nostrils flared, the look of pain wiped away.

"I *refuse* to let you do that!"

Ah, there was the anger. I rubbed a hand across my face and pushed off the bed to sit up. "You don't have a choice, love."

Mira closed her eyes for a brief moment, as if to steel herself. "I've worked very, *very* hard to be able to support myself. You can't just take that away without even consulting me." She spoke through gritted teeth, as if she was just barely hanging on to her composure. I was mildly surprised that she bothered trying.

"Well, now you don't have to work hard anymore. At least you'll get *something* good out of this deal." I swear, it was meant as a silver-lining sort of point, but from the way her eyes flashed with renewed anger, I took it I'd failed to get that across.

"You arrogant bastard," she hissed. By her sides, her knuckles were turning white, she was clenching her fists that hard. "You have no idea the lengths I've had to go to to be independent. Do you have any idea how impossible it is to get out from a crime family? No, I bet you don't—I bet the thought that there could be more to life than violence has never even crossed your mind! Do you think I just waltzed into my line of work? That I changed my name just because I felt like it? Just try to imagine how your big mob father would react if you said you wanted nothing to do with his business. Just for one second, picture it. What would he do?"

I paused as her scathing words dug deep into my skull and anchored down. What my father would do if I'd turned my back on the family business in any way, shape, or form? He'd have me killed, simple as.

"Everything I've wanted, everything I've done, has

been to be free from it all. So no, you forcing me to quit working is not '*something good*' to come out of this, Blaine. It was the last thing I had left!" She sent me one final look of anger and resentment, and then she spun around on her heel and left my room, slamming the door behind her.

I stared at the closed door while her voice echoed in my head. For the first time in as far back as I could remember, my own temper hadn't flared while someone shouted at me. I felt a lot of things, but anger wasn't one of them. Frustration, sure, along with a highly unfamiliar urge to apologize.

I shook my head in an attempt at clearing it of the odd sensation. It wasn't like it was my fault—if I allowed her to go to work, she'd likely get killed or kidnapped within two weeks. It wasn't happening.

Great. Why did I have to get married to the only woman I'd ever met who wasn't interested in the lifestyle that came with being by my side? I'd fucked countless girls who would have happily traded in their day job for my MasterCard and playing lady of the house, or whatever the fuck women did at home all day. And I'd damn sure get morning sex to boot.

Of course, none of those girls had clawed their way out from a family like the Clerys, only to get dragged back in once they thought they were free.

I grunted at the unwanted pang of empathy for my temperamental wife. It couldn't be easy, seeing everything she'd worked for disappear practically overnight. It would have taken a lot of guts to give her family the slip, and realizing it'd all been for nothing had got to sting.

I'd never wanted to be free from it all. Sure, my life was violent and bloody, but I liked it that way. Most of the time.

If I'd ever wanted something else, though... would I have had the guts to cross the family? Knowing what would likely happen if they found me again? Probably not.

She was tough as nails, that bird. She didn't look it, but defying a family like the Clerys took more balls than most grown men would be able to muster. Including me.

I couldn't give her the freedom she wanted, but perhaps it didn't have to be like this, either.

Maybe we could figure something out, so we weren't both so goddamn miserable all the time. A truce, of sorts.

***

"MIRA?" I gave the wooden door to the room she'd picked a cursory knock, but didn't bother waiting for her to answer. She'd walked into my room without so much as a knock, after all.

She was sitting on the bed in a nest of ruffled sheets and blankets, and the look she gave me was sullen. It softened notably when she spotted the large pizza box in my hand.

"Hope you like Hawaiian." I walked over to her bed and sat down without being invited, plopping the box between us.

"I hate pineapple." She reached for the box as soon as it touched the blanket, her fingers wedging it open with skilled ease.

"If you'd stuck around, I'd have asked what toppings you like." I grabbed a slice of the cheesy goodness and leaned back on one hand to watch her while I ate.

Mira didn't look up, but I saw a small grimace pass over her face before she began picking pineapple off a slice of pizza. "Sorry. I shouldn't have done that."

I assumes by *"that,"* she meant yelling at me and slamming the door. I shrugged. "It's a shitty situation. I get it."

She sighed and nodded, never taking her eyes off the pizza.

We ate in silence for a good twenty minutes, but I didn't mind the lack of conversation. I spent the time looking at her, much like I would usually evaluate an opponent before a fight. She looked so soft and fragile, but there was clearly steel underneath it all. And she was smart. I'd seen the fancy university degree hanging on her office wall, and the way she held her own in every argument we'd been in was something new to me. It was also half the reason I couldn't stop thinking about shagging her. I had no idea what it was about being bitched at that got me rock-hard, but clearly it did something for me, since just the thought of her smart mouth made my cock stir.

I shifted on the bed, strategically placing a stray pillow across my lap. Somehow, I didn't think an offer of a quick romp would ease the tension between us.

"I don't normally act like this."

I arched an eyebrow at her. "No?"

"No." She sighed, finally raising her gaze to meet mine. "I know you didn't want this either. I just... I don't know what to do."

"There's not much *to* do." I reached over and grabbed one of her leftover pieces of pineapple from the cardboard and popped it into my mouth. "It is what it is, and we can't change that, much as we want to. So the way I see it, we have two options open for us. Either we continue bickering every chance we get, or... we try to get along as best we can. I figure if we pick option two, maybe we'll be just slightly less miserable."

She snorted and a flicker of amusement pulled at the corner of her mouth.

"What's funny?"

The flicker turned into a full, albeit wry, smile. "Just that I'm failing miserably as a psychologist, what with leaving the calm rationalization up to the thug in the room while I'm busy freaking out. The irony is sort of poetic."

I raised both eyebrows at her in mock-insult. "*The thug?*"

Mira waved a hand dismissively at me. "Thug, crime lord, mobster. Take your pick."

I chuckled. "I almost want to see you call my father a '*thug*' to his face."

She sighed again and looked at me, this time with a questioning frown that made her look oddly innocent. My cock gave a spasm in agreement of my assessment.

"Do you think we can make it work?" she asked.

"What, the marriage?"

"The trying-to-get-along-thing," she said quickly. "I'm under no illusion that it'll ever be an actual marriage, but... maybe if we can figure out to just get along, that'll be enough."

I gave her a small smile. "Yeah, I think we can try that."

Getting along would be a massive step up from what I'd envisioned my future with her to be like just this morning, yet when I left her room to get on with my night shortly after, it wasn't relief that made me draw in a deep breath before I headed for the stairs.

If "getting along" was much more than what I'd been hoping for this morning, then why was part of me disappointed that she'd made it so clear she had no intentions of making the marriage work?

TEN

MIRA

Sharing that pizza was the last time in more than a week that I saw Blaine. Sure, I'd occasionally hear him banging around in the kitchen when I was in my bedroom, or hear his shower going while I trotted down the stairs to the kitchen myself, but we didn't actually come face-to-face at any point.

At the beginning, I found it such a relief. Not actually seeing him meant I didn't have to really deal with him, which made getting along so much easier. I talked to Rob—the goon who was most frequently stationed outside our front door—and got my shopping arrangements sorted out, and was on that occasion handed the platinum AmEx Blaine had apparently told his right-hand man to give to me with instructions to use it as I pleased, "within reason."

I'm not going to lie, the "within reason" part only lasted until I'd opened up John Lewis' website.

My job as a psychologist allowed me to get by just fine, but I'd never before been in a situation where I could get all the furnishings I dreamed of with just a few clicks of a button. It was completely intoxicating.

I spent a full week in an online shopping frenzy, which I vaguely justified with my plan to befriend Blaine. It was obvious that he expected me to be a good little homemaking mob wife, and as long as that only involved buying pretty things with his money, I was happy to play the part.

Only, on the ninth day, when most of my purchases arrived at the door, Blaine was nowhere to be found.

"Where is he?"

Rob gave me a short glance over the top of the gold-striped sofa he and his partner for the day were in the process of dragging through the hallway and into one of the reception rooms. "Out."

"Out where?" I followed the two men, ensuring they put the sofa where I'd specified.

"Working. Here?"

I nodded, and the two goons put the sofa down on the new rug in front of the heavy coffee table they'd carried in before.

"When will he be back?"

"Dunno." Rob rubbed his lower back with a sigh before heading back toward the hallway, no doubt eager to get done with dragging furniture for me as soon as possible.

I plopped down on my new sofa and bit my lip as the flaw in my plan finally dawned on me. While Blaine not being around meant I didn't have to deal with him, it also meant that I was nowhere near my goal of befriending him. And if he didn't hang around long enough that I could make him trust me, then there was zero chance he would ever give me enough rein that I could eventually escape.

I'd thought that getting all domesticated and making our house into a home would perhaps break the ice between us—that if he saw me making an effort to be more like what he wanted from a wife, he would be easier to manage.

But if the bastard wasn't even home to notice, then my plan wasn't going to work.

I looked up as Rob and Greg came, huffing and puffing, through the open French doors into the reception room with a seven-foot bookshelf made from solid oak, sweat beading on both their foreheads.

I hadn't talked much to either of them or the other men who played bodyguards in front of our house, apart from when I needed to have them approve the lists of companies where I'd ordered food and furniture from.

They scared me. Everything about them, from their tough faces, bulging muscles, and unapproachable demeanors, reminded me of the darkest parts of my childhood. I had learned to fear men like them from an early age, as much as I'd learned to fear their superiors, like Blaine and his family. Yet, when I looked at them now as they dragged all my heavy purchases up and down the stairs, to make sure everything was just as I'd asked, it was easier to see them for more than something to be scared of. They were busting their arses to make me happy, even if they did it with grim expressions and only because Blaine undoubtedly had told them to help me out whenever I asked.

A wave of gratitude swept over me when I saw Greg wince as they sat down my heavy book case. Babysitting your boss's wife would have to suck pretty hard, even if your day job was being a criminal, and yet they did it without making me feel like a burden. Granted, they didn't exactly make me feel warm and welcome, either, but then again, *I* hadn't done anything to make *them* feel welcome.

"Would you like a cup of tea?

Neither man managed to hide a look of surprise as I stood up from the sofa and offered each a genuine, if somewhat tentative, smile.

"Uh. Sure. Thanks."

"It's the least I can do, for all the work you've done for me," I chirped, suddenly in a much better mood. Perhaps it was because it was my first positive interaction with another human being in weeks, but the simple act of putting the kettle on and getting the fancy china out I'd bought a few days ago made me feel like a different person. Or a real person, I should say, rather than a depressed captive with access to the Internet and a shopping addiction.

I made the tea in my new pretty, pink-and-green pot and arranged three cups on a silver tray. Then, thinking about all the hard work Greg and Rob had been doing all day, I threw together a few sandwiches as well, but when I went to put them on the tray I realized that I likely wasn't going to get many other chances to break out my Butterfly Bloom afternoon tea set.

Fifteen minutes later, I'd set up the three-tier cake stand and filled it with sandwiches, store-bought scones and some cakes I'd planned on eating later in my room, and the kitchen breakfast bar had been transformed into a full-on tea party.

"Tea's ready," I yelled up the stairs, where I'd last heard the two bodyguards bump around with yet another piece of bulging furniture.

From the looks on their faces when they entered the kitchen thirty seconds later, they hadn't expected the colorful spread.

"This is for us?" Rob's one eyebrow was quirked in what I could only assume was mild disbelief.

I felt my face heat up a bit. Okay, so maybe I'd gone a bit overboard. "Yeah... I figured you might be hungry, and..." And it wasn't like I would be able to invite anyone else over for tea and scones anytime soon. Not that I was the most social of people, but a full week in near-isolation had apparently made me pretty starved for company. I sat down on the bar stool farthest left and grabbed a sandwich triangle—crust free. "Help yourselves."

Both men sat down with some hesitation, which only emphasized how much their rough appearance clashed with the delicate porcelain.

"You don't like afternoon tea?" I guessed, doing my best to keep the disappointment out of my voice. Just because I was desperately lonely enough to try and socialize with Blaine's hired goons didn't mean that they had any interest in making even the most basic of smalltalk with me.

"No, it's fine. Great, even," Rob hurriedly replied, and I got the feeling I hadn't kept my disappointment very well-hidden. He grabbed a sandwich himself and took a big bite. His hum of enjoyment seemed more genuine.

"We're just used to Blaine," Greg said, a wide grin spreading on his face as he picked a buttered scone off the cake stand. "The most you get out of him is a luke-warm beer after a hit."

I paled at the reference to the *other* part of their job, but caught myself before I could freak out. I knew what they did—being a delicate flower about it wasn't going to do me any good right now.

Rob gave him an elbow to the side. "Don't talk about

that in front of a lady, eh? She don't wanna hear it."

"It's not like she doesn't know," Greg muttered.

Rob rolled his eyes—a move that looked surprisingly comical due to his general physique. It's not often you get the delight of seeing a six-foot tall, four-foot wide criminal wearing a leather vest roll his eyes like a teenage girl. "You'll have to excuse him. He's never held on to a lady friend long enough to know the basics."

Greg gave him a baleful glare and muttered what were undoubtedly profanities under his breath, but I latched on to the conversation changer with both hands.

"And you? Have you got a girlfriend?"

"A wife, going on five years now." His face lit up with pure reverence, and I found it impossible not to instantly like him a whole lot more. A man who lit up like a Christmas tree at the mention of his wife had to have some good qualities tucked away, no matter his chosen profession. "And two wee ones, four and two."

I smiled at his obvious pride. "Boys or girls?"

"One of each." Rob took a sip of his tea and his gaze turned somewhat sly. "What are you hoping for? Once you and Blaine get to the baby-making?"

I choked on the tea that'd been on its way down my throat. Greg helpfully thumped his fist against my back, making me cough and spit the offending liquid up.

"Uh... yeah, I don't think there'll be any babies in our near future." I got up to get a paper towel, using the spillage as an excuse to turn my back on them while I got my breathing under control. Just the thought of raising a child with Blaine made every hair on my body stand on end. It wasn't that I didn't want kids, per se, but in a forced marriage to a criminal I was planning on running away from the first chance I got? No thanks.

"Pity. I'd like to see Blaine with a couple of rugrats." Rob chuckled and winked at me "Think it'd do him some good."

I managed a smile. "I take it it straightened you right out, then?"

Greg guffawed. "I don't know about straightening him out, but he did blow a big heist because he insisted on swinging by a pharmacy for the kid on his way to the checkpoint. Months of planning down the drain. Blaine nearly took both our thumbs for it."

Rob's ears reddened until they were nearly the same color as his ginger hair. "Penny had an ear infection. What was I gonna do, not get her the meds she needed? Just you wait until a lady is dumb enough to let you put a baby in her. You'll see your priorities straightened out right quick, too."

I lost track of time as I sat with the two bodyguards. They told me a few stories about their crew, and despite knowing what they did—even if they spared me the illegal details—I found myself genuinely enjoying the chat. Perhaps it was because I'd been so starved for company, but the more I listened, the more I realized that both men were actually decent people. They were warm and sometimes funny, and it was obvious they saw each other and the rest of their crew as family.

Despite having grown up in a family similar to the Steels, I'd never known this type of bonding to occur within the ranks. It had always seemed like my father ruled his employees with fear and threats, and every one I'd met before I ran away had been mean and scary.

It surprised me to find that Greg and Rob obviously had plenty respect, and perhaps even a measure of fear, for Blaine and his family, but both seemed to have a loyalty to the Steels that went beyond the threat of their power.

A point that was proven just before six when the sound of the front door opening and shutting made both men reach behind them to what I guessed were their concealed weapons, but when Blaine appeared in the doorway to the kitchen, they both returned to their tea and cake with a casual "Hey, boss."

Blaine took in the scene in front of him with first one, and then—at the sight of the now raided cake stand —both eyebrows raised. "I see you're having a tea party, rather than guarding the front door."

Rob shrugged and swallowed the final bite of his cake. "You said to look after the lass. Ain't no reason we can't do it from in here."

"I offered them tea," I added. "They've been helping me carry all the furniture in."

He turned his head then, and I swallowed automatically under the weight of his full attention. It was the first time we'd even been in the same room since we shared that pizza and agreed to try to get along, and it would seem all the time apart had made me forget just how intense his presence was.

After everything that happened with the wedding and the night that followed, I'd been too emotionally unstable to dwell much on our drunken mistake. But seeing Blaine now, after a week of getting to terms with my current situation, brought everything that had happened that night rushing to the surface. Every touch of his hands against my skin, every moan and every thrust played out for my mind's eye in high-definition while I stared at him, until I could feel my own pulse in my cheeks, my blush was that impressive.

Why, *why*, had I not just left the bed before things got out of hand? It had been hard enough to deal with him when I could still deny my rampant attraction to him—now that he knew just how much my body reacted to his, I found it near-impossible to look him in the eye.

Blaine seemed to notice my flustered state, because his soft lips pulled up in a devious sort of smirk. "So I see."

What was *that* supposed to mean? I rubbed at my neck, irritated that I let myself get so affected by him. With as much dignity as I could muster, I turned away from him to face the two bodyguards. "Do you guys want to stay for dinner? I was going to make lasagna."

"No thanks, love." Rob stretched his arms out before getting off the bar stool he'd been perched on for the past few hours. "The missus's expecting me home soon, and Greg's got another job to get to. Thanks for tea, though."

I tried to hide my disappointment. It had been so nice not being alone all day. "Well, thank you for helping me today. See you tomorrow, then."

I walked them to the door and sighed when it closed behind them, leaving me alone in the hallway. Guess I could always spend the night reading. Again.

"I'll have a bite of that lasagna."

Startled, I spun around and blinked in surprise at the sight of Blaine's looming figure. He was leaning against the doorway to the dining room, with the same little smirk playing on his lips. "That is, if you don't mind the company."

ELEVEN

MIRA

"I thought you'd gone upstairs."

It wasn't the brightest of comments, seeing as he obviously hadn't disappeared up to his room as he usually did the second he got in the door, but it just flew out of me before I managed to stop myself.

"Well, I didn't." He crossed his arms over his chest as he straightened up a bit, making the leather of his black sleeves tighten over his muscles. "So maybe we can give the new dining table you bought a spin, eh?"

Huh. I nodded and attempted to straighten out my frown. It was funny, really. I'd found it easy enough to relax around Rob and Greg today, but something about Blaine just put me on edge, as if his mere presence disrupted the magnetic charges in my body, yet I was pretty sure my two bodyguards had just as horrible crimes on their consciences as my new husband did.

"Okay, I'll... call you when it's ready."

"Need a hand with anything?"

I blinked twice before I managed to pick up my jaw. Had Blaine Steel just offered to *help* me? In the kitchen, of all places? Not at all something I would have expected from the bad boy stereotype he otherwise seemed to fit so perfectly.

"Er, no thanks, that's all right. It won't take me long," I finally managed. "Thank you, though."

He shrugged and turned around, leaving me to stare after him as he disappeared up the stairs.

As much as I'd been surprised by Blaine's offer, I desperately needed some time to get myself together again before I spent any length of time with him. This was the first time I'd get a chance to work on getting him to eventually trust me, and I needed to keep my wits about me for that.

I spent the time the lasagna was in the oven on setting the new dining table as prettily as I could. I was pretty sure Blaine's offer of eating together came from seeing my efforts to decorate the house and be a good little homemaker, so I wanted to nurture that part as much as possible. Thankfully, I'd bought some really pretty plates from an antique store with an online shop to go with the tea set, so the table had a nice splash of color even though I'd not thought to get any flowers. I briefly considered popping into the garden to cut a few of the last autumn blooms I'd seen through the window, but decided against it since it was already too dark to see much.

Instead, I placed some of the candles I'd bought around the window ledges and on the table. Once they were lit and the food was on the table, I stepped back to admire my handiwork.

The lasagna smelled gorgeous, and the candles sent a warm glow through the room, emphasizing the colorful plates and intimate atmosphere I was hoping to bring out. Yup, this looked exactly like something a dedicated wife would set out for her hardworking husband. Part one of my plan was complete.

I went to the stairs to call for Blaine, and then went back into the dining room and took a seat. I felt oddly nervous as I waited for him—but of course, my entire future did depend on this going right. I wiped my sweaty palms on my jeans just as Blaine came in, and offered him a smile I hoped didn't reflect my nerves.

He looked around the room slowly, from the candle-light reflecting off the dark windows to the set table, and finally to me.

"I got a few things," I said, worried he'd mind all the money I'd spent on decor. "To make it more homey."

"Yeah, I saw the credit card statement." He sat down on the opposite side of the table. "Food looks good."

Of course he had checked what I bought. I bit my lip, suddenly regretting my week-long shopping spree. "I'm sorry if it was too much."

"It's fine." Blaine grabbed the serving knife and cut a large slice out of the lasagna. He followed up with a generous helping from the salad bowl and then handed me the plate. "To be honest, I'm surprise there're not any expensive handbags or shoes on that statement."

I took the plate he was handing me, too surprised with his statement to wonder why he was plating my food for me. "Uh, I'm not expecting you to pick up the bill for my clothes shopping."

Blaine sighed, pausing with his hand on the serving knife in the middle of cutting out his own slice of lasagna. "Can we please not have another fight about how you want to be independent? I'm your husband, and you can't work—I'll be paying for your clothes, along with the household supplies and anything else you'll need."

"Oh." A part of me did want to argue, to lament on how this whole arrangement was fucked up and how I wanted to be able to support myself. But that would have defeated the purpose of the night, so instead I just sent him a sweet smile. "Gotcha. I'll be sure to add a few pairs of Louboutins to next week's shop. To make you happy, of course."

Blaine snorted as he returned to filling his plate. "Cheers, love. Appreciate it."

His dry tone made an unexpected snicker burst out before I could stop myself, but when I glanced at

Blaine's face, a mildly teasing smile touched his soft mouth.

"So you *do* laugh. I was beginning to wonder."

I raised my eyebrows at him. "Yes, I've been dragging your good mood right down with my sulking, haven't I? And you, who are nothing but easy smiles and giggles."

The corner of his mouth quirked up higher. "Sassy 'til the end. If you're not careful, I'll start to enjoy your lip."

"Hmm," I hummed, returning my focus to the food when I could feel my face heating up again. Getting any sort of proper conversation started was going to be really difficult, if I couldn't even keep eye contact without lighting up like a fluorescent tomato. Not for the first time, I silently cursed at my inability to control my ovaries' inexplicable freak-outs around Blaine Steel.

But if I wanted to get him to trust me, then I needed to talk to him.

After about five minutes of the only sound in the room being the scraping of cutlery against plates, I looked back up at my dinner companion. He didn't stop eating, but I could tell from the way his eyebrows shot up that he was aware I was looking at him.

"So... are any of your brothers married?" It was the first thing that popped into my head, partly because the only time he'd been even remotely open with me before was when he'd mentioned his family in our session.

"Didn't take you for the smalltalk type, Mira." He didn't look up from the meal as he spoke, but his voice didn't carry any note of warning, so I figured it was a green light to proceed.

"You said yourself we should try to get along, and it's a lot easier if we know a bit about each other, don't you think?" My own tone was light and calm. Why was it so much easier to act like an adult rather than a hormone-addled teenager as soon as he wasn't looking at me? "Besides, it doesn't have to be small talk. I may not know much about you, but I do know your family is important to you."

He finally looked up then, a sharp gleam of something dark in his storm gray eyes, but it was gone before I could fully process it.

"You know how it is. Family is everything in this business. And no, none of my brothers are married. I was the first to be sacrificed on the marital alter. What about you? Any of your brothers married?"

"I don't know," I answered honestly. "It's not like I've kept in touch. If you don't mind, I'd rather not talk about them."

He nodded, picking at his salad with his fork. "Sure. Guess you're pretty pissed at them for making you get hitched, huh?"

I shrugged, opting to deflect rather than respond. "So I take it you're the oldest, since you're the one who got chosen to get married off for the business' sake? You said you had five brothers, right?"

Blaine grunted. "I'm the third oldest. You would have seen Marcus and the twins at the wedding—they're all younger than me. Jeremy and Isaac were... indisposed, so I was up."

"Oh." Something he'd said in our session together niggled at the forefront of my mind, and I frowned. "You said one of your brothers went to prison. I assume that was either Jeremy or Isaac, then?"

He finally looked up from his plate then, but the anger that flashed in his steely gaze made me wish he hadn't.

And then it dawned on me—I'd referenced something from probably the only time in recent history that Blaine Steel had allowed himself to be vulnerable. *I* had witnessed a rare slip in his carefree, all-powerful façade, and it didn't take a psychology degree to know that he'd regretted it the moment it happened, the way he acted toward me after. And now I'd been stupid enough to remind him.

Perhaps an appropriate response would have been to pretend like I didn't notice the way his knuckles whitened around his grip on the fork, or the murderous glare he was leveling at me. Or maybe even outright fear and a stuttered apology would have been a good option.

In hindsight, pretty much anything other than what I did would have been a good choice.

"Oh, give me a *break*! What, so I have to pretend like I don't know one of your brothers is in jail? Is your ego really *that* fragile, Blaine?" I tossed my fork and knife down on the table, overwhelmed with frustration. "So you've got issues with your family—big deal! It's not like I'm going to tell anyone the big, scary crime lord went to see a therapist, so you can knock that glaring right off."

"You should learn respect." Blaine's voice was a low growl, the threat in his words emphasized perfectly by the deep rumble. "And I don't *ever* want to hear you talk about that again, are we clear?"

"Are we *clear?* Yeah, I guess we are. It's perfectly clear to me that you have zero respect for anyone but yourself, you sexist prick! *I* should learn respect? How about you earn it, for once in your life?" I didn't know when I'd gotten out of my seat, but when Blaine pushed back his chair with a loud screeching to stand up on the other side of the table, I realized I was already standing up myself, leaning over the table to shout at him.

"*Watch it.*" Blaine's otherwise light gray eyes were nearly black with rage as he put both hands on the table and leaned in so he could glower down at me from his much higher vantage point. "I've been more than accommodating with you up until now. Push me one more time, I fucking dare you."

I have no idea what idiotic demon possessed me then, but the next thing I knew, I'd grabbed my half-empty wine glass. My arm was midway through the slinging motion before my sanity snapped at least somewhat back, and I looked on as if watching a movie on half speed as the red wine I'd been sipping throughout the meal sailed through the air and connected with Blaine's face.

Three seconds passed in complete silence as I stared at him. My own anger was still boiling underneath the surface, but the absolute murderous rage in Blaine's eyes as he stared me down with wine dripping from his chin made me realize I'd made a mistake. A really, really big mistake.

"I-I'm sorry. I don't know why I... did that." My apology died into a whisper when Blaine slowly raised one large hand to wipe the red liquid off his face, and then cracked his neck without taking his eyes off me, or even blinking.

Survival instincts—finally—kicked in, and my brain quickly abandoned *"fight"* mode, opting instead for the much wiser *"flight"* option. I spun around on my heel and practically threw myself across the dining room, grabbing on to the door frame to turn the corner as fast as possible.

Behind me, the loud screeching of a chair being kicked out of the way made my already frantic heart jolt into overdrive. Its pounding against my ribs matched my feet's pace as I ran as fast as I could down the hallway to the stairs. I didn't think of what would happen once I reached my room—all I knew was that I needed to put as much distance between myself and the lethal killer chasing me, and that one room was the only place my panicked brain connected with any shred of safety.

I made it to the top of the first flight of stairs, but when I grasped on to the banister to reach the next level, he caught me.

Strong hands grabbed around my hips and *pulled*, and I was yanked backward so roughly I completely lost my footing.

I yelped as I flew through the air, arms flailing for purchase, and then I was on my back on the landing outside Blaine's room, my impact with the hard wooden floor thankfully softened somewhat by the thick rug I'd had Greg put there earlier today.

I didn't have many moments to be thankful for my design decision. Less than two seconds after I was on my back on the floor, Blaine crouched over me, pinning my wrists next to my head with his large hands while my lower body was strapped down by his knees. I was trapped.

"Let me go!" I pulled uselessly on my hands and tried to shift my hips to throw him off me, but I might as well have tried to dislodge a boulder.

Blaine growled, sounding so much like an enraged animal that I couldn't hold back a small whimper. He was so much stronger than me, he could rip me apart with his bare hands if he wanted—and right now, it very much looked like he wanted.

Yet deep down, something in my core—something undoubtedly really stupid—didn't believe he would actually hurt me. The startling moment that thought rooted itself in my stomach was strong enough to pull me out of my fear

Blaine stared down at me, his chest heaving as hard as mine and his face drawn in a mask of anger. And suddenly, it all seemed so completely ridiculous. I, a trained psychologist, for crying out loud, had resorted to throwing wine in a man's face. And he, a scary-ass criminal, had chased me down and was now pinning me to the floor. We seemed to have reached a thorough stalemate.

The amused giggle slipped out of my mouth before I managed to stop it.

"Sorry, sorry," I gasped in between my still labored breathing. My giggles died down as I stared up into his dark eyes. Behind his fury there was something else. It took me several seconds to realize that it was a glimpse of what lay behind his normally impenetrable shields. For a few, short moments, I saw past the smartarse, the ruthlessness he normally wore like a mask.

It only lasted a few second. Then raw and unbridled lust washed away anything and everything else, and his lips crashed against mine.

TWELVE

MIRA

Blaine's kiss was rough and wild, his lips bruising in their all-encompassing need.

It wasn't enough.

I kissed him back with equal strength, biting at his lip as he pushed his tongue in between mine, fighting him for dominance. The heat of his mouth was intoxicating, and all I could think of was getting more of it—more of *him*.

Our tongues tangled and I moaned at the first brush. *Yes, just like that—*

He pressed down on top of me and in between my legs, and I felt the heavy weight of his cock straining against his jeans just where I needed it as he ground against me.

Yes, yes, yes! My body sang as my clit pulsed from

the stimulation, and I rocked up against him to meet his thrusts.

Blaine groaned into my mouth and released my wrists.

I immediately latched onto his shoulders, pulling his chest down on top of me. I wanted to feel all of him against me, wanted all of his heat to consume me—

The unexpected touch of Blaine's hand against my abdomen ripped me out of my hazed lust more efficiently than a bucket of cold water would have.

I pulled my head back from his kiss with a gasp and looked down. He'd shoved my shirt up high, exposing my soft stomach to his hungrily roaming eyes. And my scars.

"Stop it!" I let go of his shoulders and thrust both hands down in front of me, pushing my shirt down to cover me again before I scrambled to scoot out from underneath him.

Blaine froze, his expression turning from wild lust to confusion—and frustration. "What?"

"You can't just paw at me like a wild animal every time we get into a fight!" I finally managed to get out from underneath him so I could sit up, clutching my crumbled shirt tighter to my body as I glared at him. The inexplicable wave of lust was—mostly—gone, replaced by anger and fear once more. Though this time, it wasn't Blaine that caused my hands to shake as they clutched at the fabric of my shirt. It was my own reactions to him—how I couldn't seem to trust myself around him. One minute I was pushing him far beyond the edge, even though I knew full well it was a stupid thing to do, and the next I was writhing in helpless surrender underneath him. And this time, I didn't even have the alcohol to blame for my erratic behavior.

No, it was becoming increasingly obvious that, for whatever reason, my brain switched off whenever I was around Blaine Steel—and *that...* that terrified me to my very core.

"*Me?*" Blaine pulled back, his upper lip curling with renewed anger. "You were not exactly an unwilling participant, were you?"

"You chased me through the house and tried to have your way with me on the goddamn floor!" I hissed, hating that he knew just how much I'd wanted it. "Tell me how I had a choice in the matter!"

Blaine's eyes darkened. Abruptly, he stood up, leaving me alone on the soft rug. "Fine! If you want to pretend like you're a bloody victim, that's up to you. I'm done with your bullshit." With one final glare in my direction he started down the stairs. Less than twenty seconds after the top of his head had disappeared down them, I heard the front door slam.

Slowly, I gathered myself up from the floor and wiped irritably at my cheeks. There was no need to cry —I'd wanted him to leave me alone, and he had.

Gingerly, I put a hand to my stomach and traced the

scars through the shirt. I couldn't feel them through the fabric, but I knew their jagged lines by heart.

Past lovers had asked me about them, and I'd lied and said they were from extensive surgery when I was a kid. Blaine would undoubtedly know what they were from a single glance. Heck, he'd probably been the cause of similar scars in his line of work.

The thought of him knowing what had been done to me made me sick with fear. Because the second he knew, he would know that I was weak. A true victim. And I knew what men like Blaine did to the weak.

I swallowed thickly and dropped my hand from my midsection. I had to stop letting him get under my skin like this. I'd thrown *wine* at him, for Pete's sake, after goading him on a subject I knew was sore.

Was it my desperate need to show him I wasn't weak? Or was it... I hesitated to even think the thought through, but dug my nails into my palms to steel myself. Was it that some shameful part of me wanted him to lose control and take me like he had that night at the hotel?

As much as I wanted to, I couldn't deny my physical attraction to him, and the sex had been...

I shook my head when I felt myself redden at the memory, angry that I let myself be so affected by Blaine's—granted, godlike—physique. I wasn't some blushing teenager who had never seen a man naked before. I had to control this—like I had to control my messed up relationship with Blaine.

Trying to befriend him was obviously not going to work out before I could figure out exactly why I was acting like I was around him, so I had to find another way to make him respect me.

I glared balefully down the stairs where he'd disappeared not that long ago. Clearly, there was a huge power difference between us, and when he could run off whenever he didn't want to deal with me anymore, and I couldn't, then he had no need to respect me.

But if I wasn't here when he came home...

My glare turned thoughtful as a plan slowly began to come together in my mind.

CONSIDERING how much Blaine had emphasized that I needed to stay in the house and that he had guards posted to watch the front door and the perimeter, it was surprisingly easy to sneak out unnoticed.

I crawled out of one of the windows facing the back garden and climbed the fence to one of the neighbor's yards with the help from a garden chair, and from there snuck my way out to the quiet streets.

Even though the house was technically still in London, it was in a well-to-do suburban area, so there wasn't much of the city's noise to disrupt the crisp autumn night.

I breathed in deeply, enjoying my first breath of freedom for what felt like an eternity. I briefly considered just running away tonight, but my passport was safely locked in a bank deposit box across town. I wouldn't be able to get to it before the morning, and by then the Steels would long since have noticed I was gone. I would never make it out of London. No, when I escaped for good, it would have to be a lot better planned.

I spent about twenty minutes walking through the neighborhood, so I was sure I could call a cab without the Steels—or worse, their enemies—getting notified. They might have their eyes on our house, but no one would bat an eyelid at a cab pulling up a mile or two away from our property.

As I walked past the big houses with their lush gardens and lit windows, I couldn't help but think about how happy I would have been to settle down in an area like this under different circumstances. It was the perfect place to raise children and live a quiet, comfortable life. Heck, I'd even spotted a few apple trees in our own garden. I could have been one of those mums who baked pies and had hot cider ready when her kids got home from school on a cold autumn day.

But that wasn't how my life had turned out, and I couldn't spend time crying about that. Not now. I had a few hours of precious freedom to look forward to, and damn it, I was going to enjoy them.

I pulled my phone out of the bag I'd grabbed before climbing out of the living room window and found the number for my favorite private hire cab company under my contacts. I gave my location, and the woman on the other end told me it'd be a ten minute wait.

I found a low fence in front of a house whose windows were dark and sat down to play on my phone while I waited. It was possibly because I was staring so intently at it that I didn't notice a black Porsche pulling up only two minutes later, until the driver stepped out.

The moment I spotted the leather-clad shoes waiting patiently on the pavement in front of me, every hair on my body stood on end. I snapped my gaze up, ready to scream for help if I needed to. Had one of the Steel's enemies seen me leave the house after all? It took a few moments for my eyes to adjust to the darkness after the bright light of my phone's display, but when they did, I recognized the stranger's dark features. It still took me a few moments to place him.

His dark hair, square jaw, and starkly handsome face looked eerily familiar, and I realized with a start that he had to be related to Blaine. He'd been at the wedding, too, standing next to Blaine and the twin groomsmen at the alter. He had to be Blaine's brother.

"M-Marcus?" I stuttered, feeling my heart calm

down a little now that I was reasonably sure I wasn't going to get kidnapped.

He nodded once and reached out a hand, clearly expecting me to take it.

I didn't. Instead, I frowned up at him. "Have you been following me?"

"No." He didn't take back his hand, instead letting it remain stretched out between us as a quiet command. "Your phone is tapped. I heard you order a cab. Was in the neighborhood anyway."

I blinked and pursed my lips. Of *course* my phone was tapped. Not like they'd let me have access to any unsupervised communication. "I take it you don't have anything better to do on a Friday night than listening in on your brother's new wife, then?"

He didn't respond—just looked at me with that same expressionless stare. It was beginning to be mildly unnerving.

"Look, I'm not going back to that house. Not yet." I crossed my arms over my chest and set my jaw. "And if you make me, I'm going to scream 'rape' so loud your eardrums will burst."

One of Marcus' dark eyebrows quirked at my threat, probably because we both knew nothing I could do could stop any of the Steels from doing what they wanted with me.

"You need to come with me. Now." Though his

voice was quiet and calm, the ring of command was unmistakable.

"Didn't you hear me? I'm *not* going back there. Your arsehole of a brother is out anyway, and until *he* asks me to come back, I'm not going."

"I will take you to my place," he said. "And I will let Blaine know where to come get you."

Something in his tone made it quite clear that this was the only deal I was going to get, and since it beat being hogtied and carried back before Blaine even realized I'd left, I relented. With a small sigh, I put my hand gingerly in his. "Fine, then."

The car ride to Marcus' place happened in complete silence. There was something dark and brooding about his presence that made my skin prickle with the sort of awareness one gets around a docile predator—alert, but not in full-blown panic mode. Not the most smalltalk-encouraging of moods.

He was different than Blaine in that way. Sure, Blaine had the "lethal predator" vibe down to a "T" when he wanted to, but his brother didn't put any effort into it. The looming *threat* I got from him was more subtle and took a while to really register, but once it did, it seemed to just roll off him in waves as if it was his natural aura.

From a psychological perspective, it was intriguing, but I found it a little hard to keep an academic distance seeing as I was trapped in a car with him. At least my ovaries weren't spazzing out like they did around Blaine.

Marcus drove us to us to an exclusive residential area in central London consisting of newer high rises made from what looked to be mainly steel and glass. He parked the Porsche in an underground basement and led me through the parking garage to a swanky looking elevator, where he proceeded to press the button for the top floor. Of course he had a penthouse.

"You're not much of a suburban kinda guy, huh?" I said with what I hoped wasn't too nervous a smile.

He glanced down at me, his expression as blank as ever, but didn't comment.

"I guess Blaine's not, either. I mean, I know he just moved into the house as well, but I can't really picture him living it up in a family home." I have no idea why I chose that strain of mindless conversation, but now that I was on it, I might as well run with it. The completely silent car ride had given me way too much time to soak in his oddly unnerving presence, so I figured a bit of small talk might help the situation.

Unfortunately for me, Marcus wasn't engaging. He kept quiet for the entire elevator ride while I chatted away about the house and the garden, motioning for me to step out of the elevator once the doors finally opened at the top floor.

Marcus' flat turned out to be as spectacular as Blaine's and my house, but for entirely different reasons.

I stopped my chattering when he ushered me in the door to stare at the breathtaking view of London's skyline through the floor-to-ceiling windows that covered the entire outer wall of the large, open-spaced living room-slash-dining room-slash kitchen we stepped into.

"This is amazing," I finally managed. I stepped all the way over to the windows and looked out. It felt like the entire city lay beneath my feet.

When I turned around, Marcus had placed a high-stemmed glass on the table and proceeded to fill it with a ruby-red wine. I raised my eyebrows in mild surprise when he held it out to me.

The large man leaned against the kitchen island next to where he'd placed the glass. An invitation to sit on the adjoining bar stool, I assumed. I gave him another hopefully not-too-nervous smile and walked back across the parquet flooring to sit where he'd indicated.

"Thank you." I took a sip from the glass, because it would have been rude not to. It felt expensive and smooth on my tongue, like thick silk. My next sip was bigger, and not from politeness.

He was watching me again, his expression as unreadable as ever.

I sighed and put the glass down. "You know, it's really unnerving when you do that."

His eyebrows rose a millimeter. I took it as a question.

"The silent staring. Or just the silence, to be honest. I think I'd prefer yelling, if this is your way of showing your disapproval."

"I offered to keep check on your phone because if my father sent someone to fetch you, you'd likely get a few bruises. I don't *disapprove* of you trying to escape. Blaine's a bastard."

"Oh." I looked up into his flint-colored eyes with some uncertainty. "Then... why didn't you just let me get in the cab?"

"Can't." Marcus looked down at the counter where he was tapping his fingers against the smooth marble. "He likes you too much."

"Uhh..." I blinked, and felt my eyebrows creep up as high on my forehead as they could go. "Who? Blaine? He said that?"

"No. Doesn't have to. We can tell."

"*'We'*?" I inquired. "And *how*? Just, you know, out of morbid curiosity. 'Cause I gotta tell ya, I'm not really getting the same vibes. In fact, I'm pretty sure he hates me as much as I hate him. A prime example would be tonight, when he chased me through the house and threw me on the floor because I pissed him off."

Marcus stilled completely, and for the first time that night, I saw clear emotion crossing his features. Dark anger filtered across his handsome face, but when he turned to face me, only his eyes kept that dark spark—

the rest of his expression was as blank as before. *"What?"*

Uh-oh. If I thought he'd had a scary presence before, it was nothing against the nearly physical tendrils of *danger* that seemed to creep across the floor and envelop the entire room with his anger.

"We had a fight," I squeaked, clutching at the wine glass hard to stop my hand from trembling. As angry as I was with Blaine, I was willing to backpedal if it meant his brother would get slightly less terrifying. "It wasn't unprovoked—I threw wine in his face."

"He *hurt* you?"

I thought back to the fight, and realized that no... he hadn't. I'd been scared, and he had been rough, but at no point had I been physically injured. "No, not really. He just... scared me. And then he left. That's why I snuck out—I wasn't planning on running away or anything. I just wanted to—to show him he can't treat me like that and expect I'll just be an obedient little woman who stays put."

I hadn't mean to confess that—not to anyone, least of all to Blaine's scary brother, but it just seemed to spill out as I stared at his blank face and storm gray eyes.

Marcus looked at me for what felt like the longest time, and I felt like he was trying to X-ray my brain with the intensity of his stare to ensure I was telling the truth. Finally, he nodded and pulled back from the kitchen counter, and it was as if the pressure in the air around us changed, making it suddenly easier to breathe.

"Finish your wine. I'm calling Blaine, and then he and I will talk before you go home. He won't ever scare you like that again."

The way he said "talk," I couldn't help but wince internally. Seemed like I'd gotten an unexpected ally.

THIRTEEN
BLAINE

"Seriously, what's gotten into you?" Liam shoved a drink across the table to me as he sat down on the crimson leather sofa on my left side. He didn't have to shout over the music, even though we were in *Red,* one of our more exclusive nightclubs. The VIP section wasn't nearly as loud as the rest of the club, set up to allow for sensitive business deals to be made in the private booths.

"Who actually *volunteers* for a liquidation job?" Louis chimed in from my right. "Even Marcus's never done that."

I looked down at my bloody knuckles with disgust. We killed people fairly frequently, and I knew even the light-hearted twins had had to put a few arseholes down over the years. Men who stole from us, enemies who crossed the line, snitches... there was always a method to it, a nearly clinical procedure that left the least amount of evidence behind. Tie the man to a chair, spread plastic wrapping underneath him, one bullet to the brain. Easy clean up.

That wasn't what I'd done tonight.

"Of course, Marcus *has* beaten more than one poor sap who crossed him to death before. Did you know the guy?" Liam asked. Despite their light tones, I knew both of them well enough to realize they were mildly concerned. I couldn't blame them. When I closed my eyes I could still feel the satisfying crunch of bones breaking beneath my fists.

"He was a human trafficker. Brought underage girls in to work for him, the sick shit." I flexed my hand and suppressed a grimace at the dull throbbing. "And I untied him—he had a fair chance."

"Right." Louis took a sip of his drink and leaned back against the high-backed sofa, sprawling out like he was completely unconcerned with my inexplicable rampage. I wished Ben hadn't called them after I told him to fuck off and let me deal with the human trafficker. If they hadn't shown up I could have disappeared into my own darkness—and right now, all I wished for was to let it swallow me up.

"But we're still pretty curious as to *why* you felt the need to go full-on Hulk. He was going to die regardless," Louis continued.

"—And you've never really struck us as the vigilante-type," Liam finished.

Fuck, those two could be annoying when you were sandwiched between them. I shot a glare first to my right, and then to my left. "It's none of your fucking business, is what it is."

"Ah."

"Mira, then."

"What did you do this time?"

"I didn't *do* anything!" I growled. "And you two knobheads need to back off right the fuck now."

"Sure you didn't." Liam gave me his driest look as he calmly sipped his drink. "Is she still not putting out, then? It's been, what, just over a week since you got hitched? Your balls must be blue by now."

"I don't care if she puts out or not," I growled. "She's not the only woman in the world. It's not like our marriage is real."

"Oh, right then." Louis gestured toward the full dance floor with his drink-free hand. "Then why don't you go pick up a bird for the night? Nothing like a good shag after a fight, right?"

I gritted my teeth and slumped back against the sofa, arms folded across my chest. Fuckers knew me far too well.

And that was the fucking travesty, wasn't it? Because ever since I'd woken up next to Mira the morning after our disaster of a wedding, I'd not been able to think about anyone but her. Just the thought of picking up some random girl made me inexplicably sick to my stomach.

But Mira didn't want me. She'd made that perfectly clear. Sure, her body reacted as strongly to me as mine did to her, but it wasn't enough. It shouldn't have mattered—she was just a bird I'd been stuck with against my will, after all. I shouldn't have given one flying fuck whether or not she wanted me.

So why did I?

I clenched my sore fist at the renewed wave of frustration that rushed through me just from thinking about her. She had brought up my family, brought up my moment of weakness, and as furious as I'd gotten, the moment she threw that wine in my face my only desire was to throw her on the table and fuck her until she begged for my forgiveness. And then again. And again.

I hated her for what she was doing to my already fucked-up mind. At least before I'd met her, the darkness in me was the only thing that'd scared me. Now... now *she* scared me, because all my thoughts and all my messed up emotions revolved around her. The one woman who refused to give in to me.

The sound of my phone ripped me out of my sulking.

Despite my frustration and generally crappy mood, a touch of curiosity made its way through at the sight of Marcus' name popping up on the display. It had been maybe a year since he last called me, and then it'd been to tell me to get my arse out of whichever girl's bed I was in at the time and meet him for a job. We saw each other regularly enough at events and jobs, sure, but we never talked much. So why the hell was he calling me now?

I flicked "answer" and held the phone up to my ear. "Yeah?"

"Your wife is at my place. Come get her."

I blinked. "Excuse me?"

"Your wife. She's with me. Come get her."

"Why the fuck is she—" I stopped talking when the call cut off and cussed under my breath. He'd never been much into phone etiquette—or any manners at all, really. Why the hell had he picked up Mira? Had our house been compromised? My gut dropped and I shot up from my seat, knocking my untouched drink over in the process.

"What's going on?" Despite Liam's relaxed pose, his shoulders tensed as he looked up at me. Ready for a fight. Out of all my father's sons, the twins were the least vicious, but I knew I could always count on them if shit hit the fan.

"I don't know," I said, already making my way out of the booth so I could get to my car. "Marcus called, said he's got Mira with him. I'll let you know if anything's going down."

"Oh. Right. You do that."

Perhaps if I'd been less focused on getting to Marcus

ASAP, I would have paid more attention to the meaningful look that passed between the twins.

WHEN THE ELEVATOR doors opened up at the penthouse floor in Marcus' building, the nervous energy in my body was so intense I had to flex my shoulders and hands a few times before I knocked on the door. If she'd been hurt, he would have said something—I hoped. But then what could have happened to make my crazy-arse brother drive all the way to the suburbs to pick up my wife? And why had he been notified, and not me?

My looping thoughts were interrupted when Marcus opened the door. His face was as blank and unreadable as always.

"She okay?" I couldn't stop the question from bubbling out. Fuck it, despite spending most of the car ride here reassuring myself, I needed to know. If not, that human trafficker wouldn't be the last person I'd kill tonight.

"Yes." Marcus stepped aside, and I walked into his well-lit flat with the view of London that would normally have made me take a few seconds to appreciate the grandness of it all. Today though, I looked around for Mira with no interest in anything else.

She was sitting by the kitchen island with an empty

wine glass next to her and a stubborn, yet somewhat unsettled, expression on her pretty face.

A knot I hadn't been aware of until then loosened in my stomach, and I drew in a quiet sigh of relief.

"Mira, go into the bedroom. Blaine and I need to talk."

I frowned at the way my brother seemed to think it was okay to order my wife around, but Mira slid off her seat without protest and pattered out of the kitchen, disappearing around a corner. Shortly after, a door clicked shut.

Huh. Seemed even my obstinate wife found it best to obey Marcus without a fight. He tended to have that effect on people, but I could have sworn Mira got off on arguing just for the sake of it.

"What?" I was aware my tone was snappy, but I didn't care. Tonight had been one long headache, and the way Marcus was eying me, I had a feeling it wasn't going to get any better anytime soon.

"She says you *chased* her through the house and threw her down on the floor. Is that true?"

I gaped at him for a moment, completely taken aback.

"Is that true?"

"Why the hell is she telling you about our business? Did you two exchange dirty details of our wedding night, as well?"

"If you ever scare her like that again, or *hurt* her, you

and I are going to have a problem. Mum would roll over in her grave if she knew you were treating a defenseless woman like this." He hadn't raised his voice, but there was an unmistakable note of warning in it.

"*Scare* her? That little tart doesn't get scared, Marcus. I don't know what the fuck she's been telling you, but that is not what went down. And why the hell do you care, anyway? Last I checked, she was my unwanted bride, not yours. If you wanted in on this shit show, you really should have stepped up earlier—saved me the headache."

"I picked her up a mile from your house. Dad's put a tap on her phone to make sure the Clerys don't fuck us over from the inside, and lucky for her, I'm the one who monitors it. She was apparently scared enough to risk the fallout of running off after your little encounter."

"Run off?" I stared at him, partly shocked that she would be that stupid, and partly impressed that she'd somehow managed to get past the security. And pretty pissed with the night team for letting her outsmart them like that. "She *ran off?*"

"Yes."

"That little..." I stopped myself from finishing that sentence at the look of warning in Marcus' eyes. "Look, I appreciate you not letting Dad find her, but you can spare me the lecture. She's fine. Now, if you'll excuse me, I have a pain in the arse of a wife to deal with."

I stepped past him, not waiting for his acknowledgment, and yelled, *"Mira!"* loud enough to resonate through the flat and into the bedroom where she was currently hiding. I set my jaw at the burst of annoyance that rolled through me at the knowledge that she was hiding from *me* behind the supposed shield of my brother's protection. She wasn't his to protect. Even if I resented the hell out of the job, it was mine, and my muscles itched with an instinctive urge to challenge Marcus for stepping in.

If I'd been drunk I might have given in, but my brain was clear enough to know that I wasn't guaranteed a win in a fight against Marcus. He'd always been completely unpredictable, and I wasn't in the mood to lose another showdown tonight. Bad enough my pint-sized spitfire of a wife had slapped me around a few hours ago, even if it was only verbally.

The door to Marcus' bedroom creaked open, and Mira came round the corner, her face drawn with tension. She stopped before she got to the kitchen area and balled her fists up beside her hips. "What?"

I bit the inside of my cheek to keep from snapping at her challenging tone. If we were going to have another domestic, it wasn't happening in front of my crazy brother. "We're going home. Now."

To my mild surprise, she didn't argue. Instead, she went over to the counter where she'd left her coat and purse, picked both up, folded the coat over her arm, and then walked over to Marcus.

"Thank you," she said softly, and then she raised up on her tiptoes and planted a light kiss on his cheek. "For your kindness."

I wasn't prepared for the wave of scalding jealousy that rushed through my veins and ended up in my chest in a molten pool of anger. Marcus. Of all people, *Marcus* was the one she thanked—for his *kindness*. If it had been one of the twins I could have accepted it, but Marcus? If I had a bad reputation, then he was the fucking anti-Christ, and yet here she was, seemingly completely at ease in his presence. And with his protection. While me... me, she treated like a bloody fiend.

I pushed the sensation down. I didn't want *her*, I just wanted to fuck her. Once I'd had my fill of her, this unbearable yearning that scratched at my insides like a thousand ants would pass, and I'd move on to greener pastures like I always did once a bird started to bore me. What did I care if she preferred my brother over me?

I held the door open for her, pretending like every cell in my body wasn't seething, and when she walked through without a word, I closed it behind us, not bothering to say goodbye to Marcus.

I'd never had any beef with my brothers before, but as I drove out of the parking lot underneath Marcus' fancy high-rise, dark resentment churned in my gut.

FOURTEEN
MIRA

We didn't speak for nearly a week after that.

I'd expected Blaine to yell at me for breaking his precious rules, but he didn't. Instead, he avoided me.

I saw him a few times in the kitchen or on the stairs, and once or twice I caught sight of him headed for the shed in the backyard, but we never exchanged as much as a word.

For the first few days, I saw it as a blessing. What had gone down between us had been way too intense, and I was happy to pretend like it'd never happened. Between Blaine's anger, my own body's treacherous reactions to his closeness and the run-in with his disturbing brother, playing make-believe was just fine by me. As much as I wanted to get Blaine to respect—and ultimately trust—me, I sorely needed a few days off from all the drama.

But by day four, the peace and quiet had lost its novelty, especially because neither Rob nor Greg, nor any of the other guards, set foot in the house unless it was to carry in my groceries. When I asked if they wanted tea or a sandwich, they always politely declined and then exited the house as if I'd offered them arsenic. It didn't take a rocket scientist to figure out that Blaine had had *words* with his men since I'd managed to sneak out without alerting any of them.

As a result, I was completely isolated, and I was beginning to go more than a little stir crazy. When I woke up on day six after *The Incident* so nauseous I had to sprint to my en-suite bathroom to throw up, I was done suffering in silence.

I leaned weakly against the toilet after the heaving was finally over, unable to muster enough energy to get off up from the tiled floor.

Great. Just what I needed—a stomach bug.

I stayed on the floor for a good half an hour, until I was reasonably certain I wouldn't hurl from moving. When I got up, my stomach lurched again, but at least the dry heaves didn't return. I quickly cleaned my teeth and then pattered downstairs to the front door.

Rob and Greg were back on watch. They both looked mildly surprised at my disheveled appearance when I opened the door, probably thanks to my checkered pajamas bottoms, silk camisole, and sleep-messy hair.

"I need crackers," I croaked. "And ginger ale." A pang from my empty stomach made me add, "And gherkins, please," before I shut the door again, not waiting for a reply. Sure, it wasn't their fault that they seemingly weren't allowed to talk to me anymore, but right then, I felt so completely alone in the world that I didn't have it in me to care whether or not it was their choice to treat me like a leper.

I felt like crap, and no one cared. Heck, if I'd somehow contracted something lethal and died, my so-called husband would likely throw a party to celebrate it.

When Rob popped in to drop off my requested goods approximately twenty minutes later, he found me hunched over the breakfast bar, crying miserably with self-pity.

"Hey now, what's the matter, love?" He sounded halfway concerned, halfway like he'd rather be anywhere else than trapped with a weeping woman, but instead of fleeing like I would have expected, he put the groceries on the counter and placed a tentative hand on my shoulder.

That one, small gesture of someone actually giving a crap turned my quiet crying into full-on belly sobs.

Rob made a startled noise at the back of his throat, clearly not having expected the Niagara Falls of snot and tears erupting in front of him.

"I-I'm so-sorry," I hiccuped, doing my best to rein in

the torrent of volatile emotions that ripped through my chest. "I'm j-just s-so alone. A-all the time."

"Mmmh," Rob hummed, as if that made all the sense in the world. It instantly made me feel a bit better, as if maybe I wasn't completely crazy.

"Tell you what, why don't you eat some of them crackers, love, and have a glass of ginger ale? I'll just give Blaine a call, have him come home to look after you."

My moment's relief vanished immediately at the sound of my husband's name. "No. Not Blaine. He h-hates me." For some unknown reason, saying it out loud made a fresh bout of tears burst out of my eyes and stain my already salt-speckled glasses.

"Nah, he's just a bit rough 'round the edges. You gotta learn to handle him. He's a Steel alright, but he's a good kid when it comes down to it." Rob gave my shoulder a light pat and fished his phone out of his pants. "You just settle down now, yeah? He'll come runnin' the second he hears you're upset."

"Don't tell him that," I sniffled pathetically. The last thing I wanted was for Blaine to know he'd beaten me with his silent treatment—especially when I felt so inexplicably weak. He didn't need to see me when I was down.

"Don't be daft," Rob said as he left the kitchen with a backwards glance over his shoulder, phone already lifted halfway to his ear. "He's a bloke—he'll crack at the sight of his wife's tears. You gotta learn to play the game, love."

I stared after the big, burly man as he disappeared out of the kitchen and out the front door. Even with my best efforts I couldn't imagine Blaine being anything remotely close to "a good kid," but perhaps Rob did have a point. Perhaps a softer touch was what was needed when it came to Blaine. I'd spent all my time trying to be strong and together—and even when I'd failed miserably, I had reacted with anger rather than tears.

Maybe he would indeed react better if he saw vulnerability in me instead.

I grabbed a piece of paper towel off the counter and wiped my eyes before blowing my nose. At least it would be pretty easy to show him vulnerability today.

WHEN BLAINE WALKED in about three quarters of an hour later, my tears had finally stopped, even if my face was still salt-streaked and my eyes red-rimmed. I hadn't been able to find the energy to go wash my face or even change into regular clothes, so when he rounded the double doors into the kitchen, he found me sitting on a bar stool still in my pajamas and snacking on a gherkin straight out of the jar.

I turned to face him when he paused in the doorway, half a pickle still in my hand. "Hey."

He frowned, his light gray eyes taking in everything from the half-empty pickle jar and used tissue on the counter to my tear-stricken face and ruffled appearance.

"What's going on? Rob said you weren't feeling well?"

From the gruffness in his voice it was hard to imagine he actually cared about my state of mind, but then again—he had come home early to check in on me, which was more than I'd expected. I bit my lip and looked down. "I'm sorry."

"Beg your pardon?" An apology was obviously not what *he'd* expected, judging from the clear note of surprise in his voice.

I managed to lift my head again so I could look at him. "I'm sorry," I repeated. "For everything that went down between us last week. It wasn't how I'd intended the night to go."

Blaine looked at me silently for a little while, as if trying to determine if I was being genuine or not. Much as I wanted to, I couldn't really blame him for his hesitance. If he'd suddenly apologized to me out of the blue, I would have suspected him of ulterior motives, too.

I put the pickle down and wrapped my arms around my midsection. Being open like this made the feelings of vulnerability come rushing back.

"I don't want it to be like this," I continued. "I know you have your family, your work, but I... I don't have anyone except you. I c-can't keep living like this, wwhere we d-don't even s-speak and..." I had to pause to not break down completely again, but I couldn't stop the tears that started to pour down my cheeks again while I tried to word exactly how alone I felt.

Blaine made a low noise at the back of his throat, something between surprise and concern. He even took two steps toward me before he paused, his hand falling to his side as if he'd been about to reach for me.

"Look, I..." His frown increased as he looked at me, obviously at a loss for what to do.

I shook my head. "You d-don't have to s-say anything. I'm s-sorry, I d-don't know what's g-gotten into me."

Blaine looked at me for a few more moments before he sighed deeply and sank down on the bar stool next to me. "I hate crying women," he muttered under his breath.

"S-sorry," I hiccuped. "D-didn't want Rob to c-call you."

"And that's the fucking problem, isn't it," he growled. "You're so bloody stubborn."

I didn't have the spirit to point out that he wasn't exactly easy to deal with, either.

Blaine rubbed his face with one hand and gave me a long, evaluating look. "Okay. Here's what we're going to do. I have a business meeting with some really important people on Sunday. They're old family friends, and I know they want to meet the new Mrs. Steel. I'll bring them home for the meeting instead, and you'll set the table and cook dinner like you did last week. If you can get through the entire night without throwing wine, I'll reconsider starting to let you get out a bit more. Show me I can trust you, and this doesn't have to suck as hard."

I blinked, sheer surprise stopping the flow of tears. It had actually... worked? Not being strong to earn his respect, not trying to be friendly to earn his trust... No, breaking down and bawling for more or less inexplicable reasons was what it took to find my way out of this mess.

"Think you can do that?" Blaine seemed noticeably more comfortable, now my sobbing had quieted down. He stretched out his long legs and grabbed a cracker from the open pack, once again the picture of an alpha male in perfect control.

I nodded and reached for another piece of paper towel. Yeah. If it meant I didn't have to go through this crushing loneliness again, then I could play his good little housewife. And who knew—perhaps by the end of it, I would also gain the key to my freedom.

FIFTEEN
BLAINE

The smell of garlic-roasted chicken hit my nostrils the second I walked through the door. Soft jazz played from the dining room, and I could see the warm glow of candle lights spilling out into the doorway, just like it had when I came down to Mira's *"Lasagna Surprise"* last week. I suppressed a cringe at the memory of how that night had ended. Hopefully, tonight would go a whole lot better. I was banking a pretty big business deal on this, and had had time to regret making the suggestion more than once since I found Mira sobbing in our kitchen in the middle of used tissue paper and clutching a giant jar of pickles. But if it worked...

I sighed softly at the memory of how vulnerable she'd looked as she sat there in her pajama bottoms and the same, silky chemise she'd worn on our wedding night. How frail. And sweet. If it worked, then maybe we could finally move forward. Yeah, I had my work and my family as she'd pointed out, but it didn't help much when all my thoughts had been circling around her for the entire past week. I hated to admit it, even to myself, but not talking to her and having the whole fucked-up disaster that was last Friday hanging over my head had been awful.

Her unexpected apology had been a godsend.

"What a lovely house. A wedding present?" Gerald Brigs, one of my father's old connections and the twins' godfather, looked around the entry hall. Next to him, his nephew, Leo, was in the process of taking off his scarf. He inhaled deeply, obviously appreciating the scents floating out from the kitchen as well.

"Ha, this is the first time I've come to your home and it doesn't smell like stale beer. New wife keeps you on a leash, huh?"

I ignored Leo and turned my focus on his uncle. He was the real power behind this deal anyway—Leo was just here as part bodyguard, part trainee. His dad didn't trust him to handle anything important on his own, and from what I knew of him, I couldn't say it was a big shock.

"Yeah, my father bought it for us. Said my old flat wasn't a place for newlyweds."

Also, he had needed it for one of his money laundering schemes.

"Mmhm, a flat is nowhere to raise little ones. They

need grass and trees." Gerald patted me on the back with a jovial grin.

I suppressed a grimace and extended an arm to lead them toward the kitchen, where I could hear Mira bustling around. If given the choice, I'd honestly rather opt for a full day of torture than have to deal with a kid, but I'd rather not burst Gerald's little fantasy of our happy home. He'd always favored doing business with men who had families, and I was keenly aware that my recent marriage was the sole reason he'd chosen to go directly through me for this deal rather than my father.

When we rounded the corner to the kitchen, it was like stepping into the twilight zone. Pots and pans were simmering on the stove, where the heavenly scent emitted from, and in front of it Mira stood, wearing an apron and a pretty dress. Her cheeks were rosy from the heat and there was a smile on her face when she looked up. Compared to what I'd walked in on earlier this week, I wouldn't have been too surprised to find that body snatchers had suddenly taken over London, starting with my temperamental little wife.

"Blaine, welcome home," she said. And then she put down the pot she'd been stirring and walked over to me where she proceeded to raise up on her tiptoes and plant a light kiss on my cheek—just like she had with Marcus.

My heart gave a weird sort of lurch. I cocked an eyebrow at her, but she just smiled up at me like nothing was amiss.

"Blaine, introduce us to your lovely wife," Gerald said from behind me, and I was jolted into motion by the reminder that we weren't alone.

"Gerald, Leo, this is Mira. Mira, Gerald and Leo. Both old family friends." More business relations, really, but to our family, it was the same—and it didn't hurt to butter Gerald up a bit.

Mira stepped forward to grab Gerald's outstretched hand and accepted his cheek kiss with that same smile on her face.

"Pleased to see you again, my dear," he said, before moving over to let Leo greet her. "I was at your wedding, of course, but I regret I wasn't able to greet you then. Forgive me, but I could have sworn the vicar introduced you as Agnes, or something to that extent?"

Mira didn't bat an eyelid. She just shrugged as she returned to the stove. "Oh, you know how it is. With a name like Aignéis, an Irish girl isn't going to have an easy time in the big city. I've been Mira for the past eight years now. You boys best get settled in at the table, the food's almost ready."

We'd never talked about why she'd changed her name, but I had a pretty good idea that it had to do with the extents she'd said she'd gone to to get out from under her family's thumb. It had obviously been a sore subject from the way she'd talked about it with me, but you wouldn't know it by looking at her now. She looked like the perfect housewife, all smiles and homely warmth as she moved around the kitchen.

With a stab in my gut I realized that she looked like my mother had, in my favorite memories of her. There weren't many wholesome family memories from my childhood, but those I had were of the times I'd snuck into the kitchen just to be around her. She loved to cook, and she was always happy when she was in the kitchen. Possibly because my father never ventured into what he classified as a woman's domain. It had always been safe, and warm.

I shook my head to clear it of the sudden onslaught of conflicting emotions. She was long gone, and getting all mushy about the past wouldn't help me land this deal.

Mira looked up at me when I left the room with our guests, an eyebrow raised in question and the warm smile replaced by a determined expression now that their backs were turned.

I couldn't hold back a wry smile of my own as I gave her a short nod—yep, no body snatchers at work here. She just wanted me to keep my end of our bargain, and was working hard to ensure I did too.

But that didn't mean I couldn't enjoy it while it lasted.

"I'VE GOT a shipment waiting to be shifted, and I happen to know you are on the lookout for a weapon upgrade for your guys." I nodded at Leo, making it clear I had my intel from a reliable source. "Why don't we hit two birds with one stone and make it part of the payment for your development site?"

Gerald leaned back in the dining chair with his glass of wine in one hand and his eyes fixed on me. As much as his friendly smile was still plastered on his face, I knew from experience he was all business now.

"Son, are you even ready to delve into developments? You and your brothers do nightclubs, small business protection, drugs... that sort of thing. And you do it well. This scene... it's for the big boys."

I gritted my teeth to stem my irritation at his patronizing tone. "Oh, I'm ready. Which I'm sure you're aware of, or else you wouldn't be here. I know you're a busy man—you don't waste your time."

The corner of his mouth twitched in acknowledgment of my point. "True. I do think you have the potential—but forgive me for having a few reservations still. It's a big project, and one I've poured a lot of resources into. Whoever takes over needs to know how to grease the right palms and crack the right skulls, or else, *I'll* end up looking bad. Let's say I take your guns off you as part of the deal—how are you going to raise the last fifty million pounds?"

I narrowed my eyes slightly, letting him know I

wasn't that easy. "Forty, tops. And don't you worry about my funds, Gerald. I know how to shift assets around. And I know this is a big opportunity. Why else would you be in my home, drinking my wine and eating the food my wife has cooked for us? I want this. And you're not going to find a better deal elsewhere."

"Well, speaking of your wife's food, it's time for dessert," Mira interjected. She and Leo had been watching us negotiate for the past twenty minutes in silence, so the sound of her voice was somewhat unexpected. I frowned at her for the interruption as she stood up, the same chirpy smile she'd been wearing all night plastered on her face. "Blaine, would you give me a hand, please?"

I cocked my eyebrow at her in silent disapproval, but she just looked at me as if nothing was amiss.

"It's a bit fiddly. Come on, please."

"Go help your wife, son. We'll continue this over the dessert," Gerald said. He gave Mira a wink. "I'm afraid you have your hands full with this one, my dear. Their mother sadly didn't have enough time with them to iron out their kinks, bless her soul. She was a good woman."

"Right," I muttered, only barely managing to keep my irritation with not only the interruption, but also the second reminder of my mother for the day, out of my voice. "Let's go look at that dessert."

Mira led the way into the kitchen, and when I'd passed through the French doors, she closed them behind me quietly, as if she was trying to not alert our guests in the dining room down the hall.

"What is it, then?" I sighed. "I gotta say, I had no idea I gave off the impression of a master confectioner."

Mira turned toward me and put her hands on her hips. The smile was once again gone. "He's playing you like a fiddle."

"Hm?" I frowned. "What do you mean?"

"He's manipulating you by seeming so reluctant. Trust me, he wants to sell that development-whatever to you really, really bad. And if I were you, I'd be very careful."

"Gerald's a family friend—he's not out to trick me." I crossed my arms and leaned against the fridge. "And what are you anyway, since you think you know his sinister motives—a damn telepath?"

"I'm a trained psychologist," she huffed, clearly getting irritated herself. "And I'm very good at reading body language. I've been watching them both throughout dinner, and the way Leo is twitching and smirking, it's obvious something isn't right about this deal. But suit yourself—if you have forty million and a shipment of automatic weapons to bet on your own ego, then what do I care? I just thought you'd like to know."

With another huff, she marched over to the fridge and opened the door so I had to step away. She fished out a tray with a chocolaty looking cake and shoved it into my arms. "Here, take this in. The sooner they're done eating, the sooner they're out the door, and I'm getting to the end of my rope playing a Stepford wife to your Al Capone."

"SON OF A BITCH!"

The development site was as dark as would be expected at four AM on a November morning, but even from my vantage point inside my car on the road next to the muddy field, it was obvious that this wasn't the multi-million dollar leisure park I'd signed off on.

We'd finished the deal before Gerald and Leo left earlier that evening, but I hadn't been able to shake Mira's warning, crazy as it had seemed. It had niggled at me until I'd finally gotten in my car, picked up Louis, and driven all the way to Manchester to look at the damn site with my own eyes.

"Looks like there was some initial plans to turn the area into a hot spot a couple of years ago, but the council shot it down," Louis said from the passenger seat. He was looking at his iPhone, reading up on what I should have looked into before ever inviting Gerald over. What I *would* have looked into, had he not had ties with the family.

"What are you going to do about it? If Dad finds out you got fucked over like this, he's not going to be pleased."

"No, and that's exactly what that bloody bastard is counting on," I growled as I clutched the steering wheel to ease some of my frustration. "He knows I'd never tell Dad, so he thinks he's got nothing to fear from the Steels, even after pulling a stunt like this."

"Our only advantage is that he's got no way of knowing you already figured out the deal was a scam," Louis said, a thoughtful frown pulling his ginger eyebrows down. He and Liam were the only ones of my brothers that had inherited our mother's red hair. "So if we act quickly, before he gets time to hide that contract you signed away, we might just be able to convince him to reconsider."

"Right. And I have just the shipment of encouragement needed to make him do that, sitting pretty in a container down by the harbor," I said, flexing my hands against the steering wheel. "Get Liam to call the crew in. We have a little house call to make once we get back to London."

SIXTEEN

MIRA

I didn't see Blaine the day after the dinner party. From my room, I heard the front door shut just before midnight and assumed he'd gone out to do whatever it was he did when he was out.

But on Tuesday, just before noon, while I was resting on the bathroom floor after the morning's final round of dry heaving, thanks to the persistent stomach bug I'd seemingly picked up, a heavy knock on my door announced his return.

I jolted, managing to knock my head against the sink as I scrambled to get up from the floor. He hadn't knocked on my door since he'd brought me the truce-pizza our first night here, and a spurt of curiosity made its way through my general self-pity. Hopefully, he didn't want me to put on another dinner party—one day of playing the perfect hostess and housewife to a crime lord was more than enough for me, thank you very much.

When I made it into my bedroom, Blaine was already standing by my bed, leafing through my copy of Sylvia Day's newest book I'd abandoned on my pillow before rushing to the bathroom.

"Put that down." I felt my cheeks flush at the thought of him coming across the sex scene I'd earmarked for later return.

To my mild astonishment, he obeyed without comment, throwing the book casually on my bedspread before he turned to look at me. As he did, his dark eyebrows pulled into a frown. "You sick?"

I took that to mean that I looked about as haggard as I felt. "Just a stomach bug."

"Ah. Does that mean you're too ill to go out for a few hours?"

I gaped at him as his words sank in. He wanted to take me *outside*. As sick as I felt, there was no way I'd pass up an opportunity to get out of the house. Besides, if the last few days were any indicator, I'd be feeling better within an hour or two anyway.

"Nuh-uh, I'm not letting you back out of our deal. Just give me a moment to get dressed. I take it you're happy with how dinner went, then?"

"Yeah." He folded his arms across his chest and leaned up against my wardrobe. "You did good."

So no mention of what I'd said about this Gerald trying to dupe him in some way, then. Ah well, that'd have to be his own problem—as long as I would get a bit more freedom going forward, I was happy.

"I'm glad. Now, where are we going? Is it a jeans or a dress thing?"

The touch of what could have been a genuine smile tugged at the corner of his mouth. "Jeans and trainers. We're not going anywhere fancy I'm afraid, love."

BLAINE DROVE us out of London, where trees and farms slowly took over the cityscape. I rolled down the window of the Jaguar's passenger side and breathed the fresh air in deeply. It was a rare, sunny November day, and despite still feeling a bit queasy, I couldn't hold back a beaming smile. How long had it been since I spent any amount of time in the countryside? Even before being forced to marry Blaine, and thus getting stuck in that house, I couldn't remember the last time I'd been outside of the city.

"You look like a golden retriever." Blaine's amused voice made me pull my head back in, but even though I gave him a glare for good measure, I couldn't stop myself from laughing. I was sure he was pretty spot on, and I didn't care.

"I haven't been out of London in eons," I sighed as I

flopped back in my seat. "This is amazing. I wish we could do this every day."

"Hmm," he hummed noncommittally. I took that to mean I shouldn't get too used to impromptu picnics and sighed with resignation. Perhaps, when I did manage to escape, I should find myself a village in the countryside somewhere and settle down for a while.

After we'd turned off the motorway and had driven along windy farm roads for a good twenty minutes, Blaine finally pulled up a long driveway that led to what looked like an equestrian farm. Horses nipped at the frozen ground behind wooden fences on both sides of the driveway.

"What are we doing here?" I asked. Even though I couldn't fathom what business Blaine had to see to on a farm, I couldn't contain my excitement. I'd loved horses with a fiery passion since I was a little girl, but hadn't had much chance to be around them since I left Ireland. Hopefully, I'd be able to at least pet one before we left again.

"You'll see." Blaine looked extraordinarily smug, and I frowned as he got out of the car and headed toward the tweed-dressed, middle-aged woman approaching us from one of the stables. Whatever he had planned, I couldn't so much as hazard a guess as to what it might be.

My curiosity piqued, and I hurried to undo my seatbelt and get out of the car. When I got to Blaine and the woman, he put his arm around my shoulder as if it was the most natural thing in the world. I froze at the unexpected touch, but if he noticed, he ignored it.

"Mrs. Wallace, this is my wife, Mira."

Mrs. Wallace nodded at me, with a smile on her weathered face. "Pleased to meet you. You sure are one lucky girl, to have such a doting husband."

I blinked, too stunned to form any words in response. *Doting husband?* Just what the heck was Blaine playing at? I narrowed my eyes and gave him a hard stare as Mrs. Wallace turned back to the driveway. Blaine just gave me a smirk and pointed in the direction Mrs. Wallace had turned.

"Oh look, perfect timing. Here they are now."

I looked down the driveway and saw a horse transport slowly make its way up. A nervous knot formed in my stomach as I saw the large vehicle approach. He hadn't. Surely, he hadn't. There was no way Blaine would do something like that for me. No way at all.

When the vehicle stopped in the middle of the yard, its passenger gave a loud whinny from within. A couple of horses from the field answered it.

I did my best to shake the chills of excitement that ran down my back. "Blaine, what is this?" I said, my voice low to keep Mrs. Wallace and the driver, who had just jumped out and walked around to the back, from hearing me.

Blaine released his grip on my shoulders and shoved

both hands into his jean pockets. His gaze was fixed on the horse transport in front of us, so I couldn't decipher his expression, but his voice was calm and devoid of emotion when he said, "You warned me about Gerald. Turns out you were right."

The driver flipped the ramp at the back end of the transport down, revealing the horse inside. It was a gorgeous, white gelding.

"It's a Lipizzan. I'm told it's got a fancy pedigree, but if it's not the type you want, we can take it back and get another one," Blaine said, as casually as if he'd gotten me a necklace.

I stared open-mouthed at the horse while Mrs. Wallace untied it and led it out of the box, stopping in front of us.

"What do you think, Mrs. Steel? He's a handsome one, isn't he?"

"Y-Yeah," I croaked. "Gorgeous."

"I'll let you two get acquainted. The grooms have his box ready when you're done looking him over. Just lead him to stable six, and we'll get him settled in." She handed me the rope and walked back toward the stables, and I was left staring dumbfounded at my very own horse.

"Is he... really for me?" I managed, without taking my eyes off the horse.

"Yeah, he's yours," Blaine confirmed. "Mrs. Wallace

will be in charge of his daily care, but we should be able to get someone to drive you out here once a week or so."

The anxious knot grew until it made my chest tight with emotion I couldn't begin to name. Blaine Steel, the man I'd hated from first sight, the man who had made it perfectly clear he hated being forced to marry me as much as I did... had fulfilled one of my lifelong dreams. To say I was shaken to my core would have been an understatement.

"How did you know?" I whispered, not trusting my voice for anything louder. "How on earth did you know I've always wanted a horse of my own?"

"You said you wanted one as a kid. I assumed you likely still did, since you brought it up."

With a start, I realized he was referring to the time he'd saved me from that group of thugs and walked me to the train station. That he had actually remembered a detail like that, and put it to use to... to what, reward me for being useful? I finally managed to tear my gaze from the horse to look over my shoulder at Blaine. He looked as calm and arrogant as ever as he stood with both hands down his front jeans pockets and the black leather coat zipped all the way up. But past the façade, there was more than just the bad boy mafia son. I wasn't sure if I only just noticed it now, or—more likely—he finally let down one or two of the shields he usually kept up. Either way, I suddenly, and with a warm flood of confusing emotion I didn't dare decipher, knew that the real Blaine was in there underneath all the swagger and smugness. And he might just be a man I'd like to get to know.

I hadn't really thought about what would happen after I gave Mira that horse.

Originally, I'd gotten it because she had saved me an arse load of money—along with my reputation. Okay, so *I* saved my reputation as someone not to be messed with when I burst into Gerald's home with six other, heavily armed men and demanded he draw the contract back, but without her, I wouldn't have known it was needed until it'd been much too late. And to top it off, I'd gotten to see Gerald nearly wet his pants as he pleaded with me to spare his miserable life.

I had, of course—if I'd killed him, my dad would undoubtedly have found out how close I was to getting fucked out of forty *million* pounds, and that was not a road I particularly wanted to travel down. I might have outgrown the belt, but he had other, much more unpleasant means of punishing his employees. Lose the family that kind of money and I'd sure as hell not be worth more than a second-rung employee to him, blood be damned.

So I'd given Mira a horse, because I remembered how she'd looked when she talked about how desperately she'd wanted one as a kid. She might have meant it as a snarky commentary on what she thought I did wrong with my life, but the wistful expression in her eyes had betrayed her true desires. And I'd paid a pretty penny for it too, not so much because I cared about equine pedigrees myself, but because I wanted her to know I valued what she'd done for me.

Sure, I had some measure of ulterior motives behind that decision—mainly that she was going to sit in on all my business deals from now on, whether she wanted to or not—but also just because if I gave someone a gift, I wanted it to be good. It didn't happen that often, after all.

What I hadn't expected was the change in Mira after we came home from the stables. It was so subtle that it took me a few days to catch on to something being different, but when she knocked on my door the next afternoon to ask if I wanted anything specific for dinner, I knew something was most definitely up.

"You're making us dinner?" I asked, my eyes narrowed in suspicion at the curvy woman in my doorway.

"Yes," she said, wrapping her arms around her midsection in that way she did when she felt defensive. "Or, I'm making *me* dinner. You don't have to have anything if you don't want to. I'm not your mother."

The catastrophe that was Lasagna Night and when I'd made her cook for Leo and Gerald aside, we hadn't eaten together since the pizza that first night, and her asking me what I wanted her to make for me was definitely a first. I bit back my urge to ask her why she was suddenly being nice—and that's when I realized the small changes that had happened for the past few days, since we came back from the stables. She'd made tea and told me there was still some left in the pot when I came in the other night, she'd initiated a few small conversations when we met in the hallway, and—more noticeably —she'd smiled at me once or twice.

I blinked as the past few days' interactions suddenly slid into a new light.

Was she... trying to be genuinely *friendly*? Because of the damn horse?

"So, do you want anything, or are you just going to stare at me until I starve to death?" she snapped, effectively ripping me out of my dawning realization.

I smothered a snicker. Clearly, my snarky little wife hadn't lost her bite just yet.

"Yeah, thanks. Whatever you're in the mood for would be nice."

"Soup, then," she said, before spinning around on

her heel and walking out of my room, presumably to go cook.

I resisted the urge to follow her down to the kitchen to watch her. The thought of how overwhelmed with memories of my childhood I'd become when coming home Sunday to the smell of dinner cooking and Mira rummaging around with pots and pans was still in fresh recollection. But she was right—she wasn't my mother, and I didn't need to delve deeper into whatever fucked up Oedipus complex was happening whenever I saw her in that apron. 'Cause I'm not going to lie, I'd spent more than one night wanking to the thought of bending her over the kitchen counter and fucking the living daylights out of her while she was wearing nothing but the apron and the messy bun she usually had her auburn hair up in these days.

My cock stirred at that thought, and I sighed wistfully. If only her sudden onset of friendliness would transform into an equally sudden, acute desire to let me get between her thighs. How many horses would that take, anyway?

With another sigh I slid my hand down my pants to alleviate the increasingly uncomfortable pressure in my cock. If nothing else, hopefully I'd get over my borderline obsession with her soon, so I could at least find other women to slake my desires with. I hadn't spent this much time masturbating since I was thirteen years old, and the novelty was quickly beginning to wear off.

"BLAINE!"

The sound of Mira's irritated voice came from inside my bedroom.

After getting off to yet another fantasy of kitchen sex with my bitchy little wife, I'd headed for the shower to clean off and calm down. It had apparently taken longer than I thought, judging by the annoyance in Mira's voice.

I briefly wondered how long she'd been calling me for as I grabbed a towel to wrap around my midriff, but such contemplations came to an abrupt halt as a devious idea sprung out.

Much as she wanted to pretend like it wasn't the case, I knew for a fact that the little prude got nice and turned on from seeing me naked. And I was really fucking tired of being the only sexually frustrated person in this house.

With a devilish smirk I dropped the towel on the floor and sauntered into my bedroom.

"For God's sake, I've been calling y—" Mira turned toward me, hands on her hips and undoubtedly gearing up for a longer tirade. However, the sight of my naked body stopped her cold.

My smirk hiked up higher when her eyes traveled down my body until they got to my crotch. A furious blush rushed to her cheeks, but she kept staring at my cock as if mesmerized.

Yep. She wasn't anywhere near as uninterested as she'd spent the past few weeks pretending like she was.

"See anything you like?" I shifted my hips a bit and saw her tongue slip out to wet her lower lip as her eyes followed the movement. *Nice.* Having her look at me like this made my cock swell in no time.

Mira made a half-choked little noise and finally found the will to snap her attention away from my rapidly growing cock.

"For fuck's sake, Blaine! Put that away!"

"Why?" I grinned, taking a few steps toward her. "It's nothing you haven't seen before."

Mira retreated backward toward the door, as if fleeing from a prowling predator. She did everything to look anywhere but at my now fully hard dick. "Just—just stop it! God, why do you have to be such a prick! I mean jerk—oh, *God!*"

I laughed out loud at her flustered sputtering. It turned into a full belly laugh when she seemingly gave up on winning the argument and turned around on her heel to flee down the stairs.

"Hey, wait up, what were you going to tell me?" I called after her. "Is dinner ready, or what?"

No reply came from downstairs, apart from some loud banging of pots from the kitchen.

I was tempted to follow her down without putting

my pants on, but figured it might not be the best idea if I ever wanted her to cook for me again. Besides, my cock was already uncomfortably hard. Seeing her all flustered and trying desperately not to look at it while we were in the room most of my fantasies about her played out in would likely torture me more than it would her.

Sighing, I walked to my closet to find some clothes.

WHEN I CAME DOWN the stairs, Mira sat at the dining table, already eating what looked like tomato soup. She'd set a plate out for me as well, and a bottle of wine.

"Smells lovely," I offered as I sauntered in to take my place.

Mira didn't look at me, but I could see her cheeks turning a delicious pink again.

I grinned. "Oh, come now, love. I've put pants on—it's all safe."

She made a huffy little sound, but finally raised her head to level me with a glare. "I really didn't need to see that."

"Oh, on the contrary—I think you did." I winked at her and grabbed a chunk of bread to dip into the soup. "Gotta give you a bit of material for those late night self-loving sessions. I am your husband, after all."

Her cheeks went from light pink to a tomato red that

rivaled the soup in seconds. "Thanks, I'll manage!" It came out as a hiss, but her flaming face spoke its own truth.

My grin widened. So she did, in fact, use me as her source material to get off? Hmm. I popped the bread into my mouth while I enjoyed her squirming in her seat, no doubt regretting that she didn't just eat in her room. As much as I wanted to continue needling her, just to see how far I could take it before she snapped, I reined myself in. I did need to talk to her, and I'd rather not do it with a faceful of wine.

"I've been meaning to ask you—how often are you right when you assess people like you did Gerald?"

Mira's eyebrows shut up, probably in surprise at the change of subject. "Most of the time. Body language is pretty universal and hard to control. Why?"

"Because I've got a..." Best make it sound optional to avoid resistance. "...business proposition for you."

Her mouth flattened into a disapproving line. "I'm not going to come with you to poker games, if that's what you've got in mind."

"Always think the worst, huh? It's got nothing to do with gambling. I simply want you to come along for my business meetings. As an adviser. You can sit in while I meet with potential business partners, and give me your opinion of them after. It would be a good way for you to get out of the house. Since you'd be with me, you'd be safe."

Mira frowned, a somewhat conflicted look passing across her pretty face. "I... I don't want anything to do with illicit affairs, Blaine. If the day ever comes where I need to explain to the police how much I knew about your activities, I don't want to have to lie to tell them I had no involvement."

I nodded. That was fair enough, given how she'd tried her best to get away from this world. "It'll only be above-board dealings. You won't be privy to anything less than kosher."

"And after these meetings, we'll go somewhere else for a little bit?"

I raised an eyebrow at the excitement she was clearly trying—and failing—to hide while she attempted to negotiate with me. I might not be as skilled at reading body language as she was, but I knew I had this one in the bag. She was way too desperate to not be cooped up in this house to turn me down. However, I didn't see the harm in letting her think she had some pull.

"What did you have in mind?"

"Oh, I don't know, maybe just... browsing a few stores, some window shopping... stopping for an ice cream if we fancy. Normal things that normal people do. A museum visit once in a while, perhaps?"

I grimaced. "How about we skip the museum and catch a movie instead?"

"Can it be French?"

"No."

Mira sighed. "Fine. But no explosion-y action flicks, either."

I laughed and reached my hand across the table. She sure did drive a hard bargain. "Okay, you've got yourself a deal."

Tentatively, she reached out her own hand and put it in mine. It was small and soft, and the touch of her palm sent a pang to my needy cock. "Deal."

I wrapped my fingers around hers for the briefest of moments, under the guise of shaking on it, but really, all I cared about was feeling the touch of her skin. Why, *why* was I so desperately attracted to her? From the first time I saw her I'd wanted to bed her, but after our drunken night together, the urge to be inside of her hadn't diminished. Quite the contrary. I'd never been with a woman who made all others seem completely uninteresting, even for a short while.

Reluctantly, I let go of her hand. "What types of movies do you like? And don't even bother listing any artsy shit."

"Oh, the usual stuff. Dramas, rom-coms, an occasional psychological thriller. How about you?" She raised a teasing eyebrow at me. "And don't even bother listing any action-y shit."

I laughed at her cheek. It was nice to have a normal conversation for once, even if it was just about cinema choices. Everything had been such a battle from day one, it felt good to just have a relaxed moment together.

It made me bold enough to suggest, "Why don't we see if we can find something we both can agree to? I saw you got us Netflix, and we haven't even broken in the couch yet."

Mira looked downright shocked, her mouth hanging slightly open at my suggestion. "What, so... watch a movie together? Here? Now?"

"Yeah." It wasn't until I saw her reaction that I realized what I'd suggested. Dinner and a movie. Not only would this be the first time outside of meals and taking her to see her horse that we'd voluntarily spend any time together—it also sounded an awful lot like a date.

"Just a movie," I hastily interjected. "No 'Netflix and chill,' I promise."

She laughed when I crossed my heart. "Alright then. But I'm warning you, I'm a crier."

SHE WAS.

Mira sobbed her way through what was meant to be a "great, romantic drama," which I found so tedious I nearly dozed off midway through. She even cried through parts of the Jim Carrey comedy I put on next in an attempt to stop her tears and my boredom.

"It's not sad!" I repeated for the fifth time when the credits finally rolled over the flat screen TV she'd bought for the living room—and which should have been at least twenty inches bigger—and she dabbed at her eyes with a much-used tissue and sipped more wine from the glass she'd been nursing through the past hour and a half.

"His wife *left* him," she protested with a sniffle. "And he raised those boys all on his own."

I didn't manage to smother my eye roll. "That was at the start of the damn movie! I've literally never known anyone who could cry at a Jim Carrey movie. Is it that time of the month or something?"

Mira gave me a reproachful look from behind her tissue. "Three hours is your max capacity for not being a jerk, huh?"

"Pretty much. I'm going to put on *Alien vs. Predator*, and if you shed as much as one tear, our movie-deal is off the table. Got it?"

She wrinkled her nose at me, either at the choice of movie or my threat I didn't know, but didn't bite back. I took that as acceptance. A choice I soon came to second guess.

"I thought I said no action crap," she moaned about fifteen minutes into the movie. "This is so boring."

"I sat through *The Notebook*. I will hear no complaints. And if you're bored, at least you're not crying."

"You're such a jerk."

"We've established that. Now, shush—someone's about to have their head ripped off."

Somewhat to my surprise she did quiet down, albeit with a semi-rebellious mumble, and I became so engrossed in the movie that it took me nearly forty-five minutes to realize she'd not said a word since. When I looked back at her, she was fast asleep, all curled up against the backrest of the couch with her head in an uncomfortable angle.

Her glasses still had salt stains on them, and a piece of her hair was stuck to the side of her face. I reached out to brush it away and she murmured in response.

"Mira?" I whispered, testing to see if she was awake. No response. She was still out cold.

I looked at her sleeping face and felt something odd stir in my chest. She looked so fragile and innocent, completely at odds with the snarky bitch I knew her to be. It made me want to protect her, even if there was nothing to protect her from at the moment.

I frowned, somewhat confused by the ridiculous notion. I'd only ever had protective feelings toward my family and, to some extent, my crew. And only when there was an actual threat to them.

Perhaps it was because she was under my care. She lived in my house, and it was my money that kept her warm and fed—even if she resented it.

I reached out to stroke her cheek without knowing why I felt the urge to.

She murmured again and pressed her face into my

touch, much like a cat would. My heart took a couple of extra beats in response, but it felt good. Hmm.

As carefully as I could, I reached out to wedge one arm underneath her head and the other under her hamstrings, slowly shifting her until she was resting in my lap with her head leaned against my shoulder at a more comfortable angle.

She made small sounds of protests while I moved her, but seemed to quiet down quickly enough once I had her settled in my arms.

The press of her body against mine felt good too. She was warm and soft and solid, and she smelled like wine and woman. My cock stirred predictably, but I ignored it. Holding a woman like this, with no expectation of it turning sexual, was a new experience, and I found I liked it.

A lot.

EIGHTEEN

MIRA

The violent urge to puke out my guts ripped me from my sleep, as it had for the past many days now. I rolled out of bed and ran for the bathroom, making it to the toilet just in time.

It took me more than twenty minutes before my stomach finally settled down enough that I realized I was wearing the same clothes as I'd been in the night before, rather than my sleep attire.

I frowned at the toilet seat as I rested my forehead against it. Come to think of it, I had no recollection of going to bed last night. The last thing I remembered was the boring alien movie Blaine forced me to watch. I must have fallen asleep on the couch. Which begged the question—how had I made it from the sofa to my bed?

The only logical explanation made me pull my head

back up with surprise. Blaine must have carried me. Huh.

A dry heave made my contemplations come to a halt as I crouched over the toilet again, but nothing came up this time. Probably because my stomach was completely empty.

Maybe I should bite the bullet and go see a doctor. If it was a stomach bug, it was really persistent. And perhaps I should also stop having wine with dinner—it probably wasn't helping things.

When my stomach finally settled down again, I cleaned my teeth and changed into fresh clothes before I went downstairs to forage for my usual breakfast— crackers and ginger ale. To my surprise, Blaine was in the kitchen when I came down, sitting by the counter on one of the bar stools and eating a bowl of cereal. If I hadn't felt so queasy, I might have appreciated the way his chiseled chest strained against his T-shirt or his triceps flexed when he lifted the spoon.

"Morning," I grumbled as I shuffled to the cabinet that held my stash of crackers.

"You look like shit," he said. Just what every girl wants to hear first thing. "Are you sick again?"

"Still."

His dark brows pulled into a frown. "I'll get Rob to make you an appointment with our doctor. Are you too ill to work today? I just got a call about a meeting this afternoon."

Despite how poorly I felt, I perked up at that. I missed using my brain, and there was only so much sudoku a girl could play before going bonkers. Sitting in on business meetings might not be as stimulating as seeing patients, but it beat hanging around the house all day.

"Yeah, I should be fine in a couple of hours. Can we go look at some shops after? There's this artisan confectionery shop I've been dying to go to."

A hint of a genuine smile played over Blaine's sensual lips. "Perhaps. We'll see if you're feeling well enough."

I made a grimace at him as I sat down with my box of crackers. "Yes, Dad. And I'll also clean my teeth and look before I cross the road."

Blaine laughed and patted me on the shoulder before he got up to put his bowl in the dishwasher. "Be ready at three—I'm getting Rob to drop you off."

I stared into my box of crackers in silence for a while after I'd heard the front door close behind him. After he gave me Walter, my wonderful Lipizzan gelding, I knew things had changed between us. Nothing was said, but it *felt* different. Calmer. Like we had a mutual respect and understanding.

It was what I'd wanted, of course—to gain his respect and with it, his trust. But I hadn't expected it to feel like this. Like everything just fit into place, somehow.

Perhaps it was my frustrating, physical attraction to him that made it seem like something deeper, just because we got along now. Yeah, that was probably it—my mutinous ovaries trying to make it out like there was more going on between us so they could get a chance at throwing themselves at him again at the earliest convenience.

Traitorous little bastards.

I grabbed a cracker and stuffed it in my mouth, savoring its bland saltiness and the immediate, calming effect it had on my nausea.

Getting along with Blaine was a vital next step in my plan. I had to keep my goal in mind, or I would never be free again.

But why did my heart suddenly cringe at the thought of betraying him like that?

"SO BLAINE SAYS you're sick. You look okay though —what's up?"

I glanced at Rob out of the corner of my eye as he navigated the big Range Rover through the city streets. There was something oddly endearing about having the burly bodyguard seemingly concerned about my health, even if it was a somewhat surreal experience.

"Just a lot of nausea and throwing up. It comes in waves—right now, I'm fine and dandy."

"Mmmhm," he hummed. "Does it come at any specific times?"

"Usually the mornings. Why, do you need to know to book my appointment with the doctor?"

"Yeah," he said, not taking his eyes off the road. "It'll help. Okay, love, looks like we've landed."

I ducked my neck to look out the front window just as we drove underneath a big professional-looking building and into its parking basement.

"Blaine's got an actual office?" I asked, somewhat surprised by the grandness of the location. Somehow, I'd expected us to drive up to a seedy motel room with stains on the carpets and the blinds pulled.

Rob chuckled. "Yeah, the Steels like to keep up appearances for the law and such. We do most business meetings here. At least, the pleasant ones."

I shuddered at the implication that the *"less pleasant"* business meetings needed to be somewhere else—somewhere the law wouldn't know about.

Rob parked up and waited for me to fumble the seatbelt off so he could escort me to the elevator. He pushed the button for the fifth floor and, when the doors opened a few moments later, stepped out as if to check the floor was clear of threats. Then he nodded to me and waved a few fingers at me, motioning for me to join him.

I smiled broadly at him. "You're taking your bodyguard duties very seriously, huh?"

He snorted. "Love, if something happens to you

under my watch, I'm dead. Can't leave the missus as a widow with two wee ones, now can I?"

"I'm sure Blaine likes you a whole lot more than me," I said, patting his arm reassuringly. "You'll be fine, even if some rival family suddenly decided to burst through the Steel's office building and kidnap me for no apparent reason."

Rob gave me a long glance. "Yeah. Sure. I guess you don't know what happened to the two men who were on guard duty the night you decided to slip out?"

My heart gave an uncomfortable lurch. I hadn't even thought about it. "W-what do you mean? What happened to them?"

"Nothing they won't recover from," he said, giving me a small shrug. "But then, they didn't let someone snatch you—you went off by your own choice. Don't underestimate him, love. He's fiercely protective of you, and has a bit of a nasty temper."

I opened my mouth to ask him what the heck he meant by that, but just then Blaine walked through the door leading into the hallway and I lost my train of thought. He'd changed into a black, tailored suit that fit him like a glove and a blue striped tie, and I was completely taken aback by my own body's reaction to the sight.

My heart sped up, making my pulse hammer in my throat, and my traitorous ovaries seemed to melt in my abdomen, making my nether region clench with sudden and intense desire. To my excruciating embarrassment, I felt my panties start to dampen.

For fuck's sakes! He was just a man in a suit. Okay, an incredibly handsome and sexy-as-hell man, but still. There was no excuse for my body to react this way at the mere sight of him.

"Thank you, Rob. I'll take it from here. You go home to your family, I'll drive her home later."

It wasn't until he spoke, his voice unusually gruff, that I realized his forehead was locked in a deep frown and his gray eyes seemed darker than normal. Clearly, he wasn't happy about something.

"Sure thing, boss." Rob nodded at us before retreating to the elevator. When the doors shut, Blaine turned to me.

"Are you ready?"

"Yeah," I croaked, willing my body to calm the heck down.

He put his hand on my shoulder, which didn't exactly help matters, and guided me through the door and into a lavishly decorated waiting area, complete with a busy-looking secretary in her mid-forties.

"I had no idea you moonlighted as a respectable business man," I joked in an attempt to alleviate my own discomfort at his closeness. Even through my clothes, I felt his hand on me like an electric pulse that heated my skin and made my heart pound heavily behind my ribs.

Blaine didn't answer, but stepped back and

motioned for me to shrug out of my coat. I obeyed, and he helped me out of it and handed it to the secretary, who seemed to magically appear by his side the moment he held out his arm.

"I'll have to warn you that this might not be a very pleasant experience for you," he murmured once she'd disappeared through another door with my coat. "When my father set up this meeting, I didn't realize who the contact would be."

I looked up at him, suddenly feeling less eager about this whole arrangement. Who on earth would make Blaine Steel seem so on edge? Was there some rival mafia trying to encroach on their territory or what? "What do you mean?"

Again, he didn't answer me, but once again he put his hand on my shoulder to lead me to to what I assumed was the door to the conference room. My suspicions were confirmed when we stepped through into a room dominated by a large, oval table. Four chairs were set out, two of them empty. In the two closest to the door and with their backs to us sat two male figures, waiting.

When the one furthest to the right turned around to look at us over his shoulder, my heart dropped.

No. No, no, no.

I fought back the bile that rose in my throat when I recognized him. As if on cue, the man at his side turned, and I had to bite my tongue to swallow a whimper.

The last time I'd seen my father and my eldest brother, Michael, they had threatened me with torture if I didn't marry the mafia son they'd picked out for me.

The time before that…

It was only Blaine's hand on my shoulder that allowed me to stumble to my chair and sit down as if someone had cut the strings that held me upright. And there they sat, two of the three men who haunted my nightmares even to this day. Right in front of me, with only the table between us for protection. I clutched at the chair's armrests until my knuckles turned white and focused on breathing deeply and evenly.

They couldn't hurt me. Blaine wouldn't let them. They couldn't hurt me, they couldn't hurt me…

"I understand from the briefing my father gave that we are to hash out a deal involving the transportation of goods between Ireland and England, correct?" Blaine said from his seat by my side. He flipped open the folder in front of him, all business and in control. If I hadn't been fighting tooth and nail to keep my looming panic attack at bay, I might have appreciated the change to his normal persona.

"Yeah, that's correct, son."

My father's lilting drawl made a shudder run up the length of my spine. Just breathe. Just breathe.

"I was unaware that your connections in Dublin ran deep enough for such an arrangement? I see no problem with hashing out a deal for the Belfast port, but do you have the necessary hold further South?" Blaine said.

"With your help, we can secure Dublin no problem," my father rumbled. "That's part of what you got your wife for, isn't it? In return for your family's backing, you got my only daughter."

I could sense Blaine looking at me, but I was too busy staring at the table to return his gaze.

He was silent for two long seconds, and then I felt a light tap on my left hand that was still clutching at the arm rest. "If you'll excuse us for a moment."

I found the strength to get up when he put his hand on my shoulder, as if he somehow transferred some of his strength into my muscles by the warmth of his touch. I didn't see anything but the carpeted floor in front of me as he led me back out of the room, past the secretary and into the quiet hallway by the elevator.

Only when we stopped did he take his hand off my shoulder again.

"What did they do?"

"What do you mean?" I could only manage to raise my voice slightly above a whisper, as if my ingrained terror constricted my vocal cords. It didn't matter, though; the hallway was so silent he heard me just fine.

"The second you saw who we were meeting, you started shaking like a leaf. And you look like you're about to barf. Add a hideous, white dress and you look exactly like you did in the church. You're obviously terrified. So I'm asking you, what did they do?" There was a low, threatening quality to Blaine's voice and a tone of no-nonsense, but I shook my head. I couldn't. No one could know.

"I can't," I finally managed to croak. I looked up from the floor to plead with him, to make him stop pushing, but the sight of anger in his eyes made the tears I'd managed to keep at bay until now finally spill over.

"You can't? You're a goddamn shrink. Talking about whatever makes you this scared should be the one thing you're good at, woman. Fuck, you know about *my* shit. You know my demons are there because of *my* family. You think I've told anyone else anything about that? So tell me what had you clutching at that poor chair like it was a life rack just at the sight of you Dad and brother. You owe me that much."

"I *owe* you?" Something about his mounting anger and the darkness in his gaze as he stared me down made the dam inside me break. And for the first time in my life, it all came spilling out. "I *owe* you to tell you what they did to me? *You* want to know, the guy who had to threaten me the second you'd let me see just a *glimpse* of the real you?"

"Yes. I want to know." He kept his voice low, despite my shrieking, but the air of command was unmistakable, even through my current meltdown.

"Fine! I'll tell you, and then you can get to roll your eyes and call me a weak little victim and go in there and make your deal with those monsters! It's all about the business, I know how it goes." I pulled up at my shirt with shaking hands, ripping frantically at the fabric until my scarred stomach was on display. "My brothers held me down while my loving father cut me. That's what they did. Because I'd jeopardized the *business*. I was eighteen, and I tried to free a man they had tied up in the basement and beaten bloody. He owed them money, you see.

"They caught me doing it and made me watch while they shot out his kneecaps. And then they gave me these. I begged them to stop. Michael *laughed* at me and my father... my father said that's what I got for being weak, and now everyone would see me for the stupid little victim I was. They didn't stop until I passed out. Are we even now, Blaine? Does that make you feel better for having given me just a glimpse of what *you* fear?"

Blaine stood silently in front of me as I finished my tirade. His eyes were dark like thunderclouds and laser focused on my scars, but the rest of his face was impassive, as if carved from rock.

I let my shirt drop down, shielding the scars from his view, and wiped my eyes with my free hand. I was still shaking from the emotional outburst, but behind the shock of it all, there was an odd sense of relief of finally having shared it all with someone. Even if that someone was Blaine.

Then, to my utter surprise, Blaine cupped my cheek with his warm hand, his thumb wiping my tears away with a surprisingly gentle stroke. He still didn't say anything, but in his darkened gaze I saw the last thing I'd expected from him: fury—on my behalf.

I closed my eyes and let the simple gesture calm me. Gradually, my heart rate slowed and my breathing evened out until I was once again in full control of myself.

"If there's one thing you're not, Mira, it's weak." Blaine's voice was quiet and as dark as his gaze had been. Then he removed his hand from my cheek and I felt him take a step back, putting more space between us. "Come back in with me. Show them that they haven't broken you."

I gritted my teeth and nodded. As much as I wanted to curl up in a corner and cry until they'd left, I knew they would think me the weak victim they'd always thought me to be if I did. And I didn't want that. I wanted to be strong, not for them, but for myself. If I could do this, then maybe I could finally start healing.

Blaine turned around and led the way back to the conference room. He waited for me to sit down, but instead of following suit, he leaned in over the table, resting on his knuckles.

I looked up at him in surprise, my eyes widening at the absolute, stone cold rage in his gaze as he leveled my father and brother with a murderous stare.

"Now you listen to me very, *very* carefully, Clery. There will be no more deals made between my family and yours. Not one. Any arrangements made in the past are null and void. You understand?"

My father gaped up at Blaine, his mouth working to form some form of protest no doubt, but the shock didn't allow for any actual words to be produced. By his side, Michael had gone completely pale—Blaine's anger was a near physical presence in the room, and terrifying beyond belief, even for me who wasn't in its direct line of fire.

"You have twenty-four hours to get the *fuck* out of London and back to Belfast, or I swear I will gut every one of you like fish."

"Now *you* listen, son!" my father protested, finally finding his voice as he got to his feet. "You have no authority to make such threats. We have an agreement with your father, and you can't—"

"Did I not make myself clear?" Blaine hissed. "Get out of my city, *now*. I am a Steel, and trust me when I say that I have all the authority I need to slaughter every last member of your miserable little gang."

"You've made a grave mistake today, boy," my father growled. He grabbed Michael by the shoulder and my brother got up from his chair too, despite looking like he was about to wet himself. "And *you*." He pointed his finger at me, and it took all I had not to shrink back from the absolute hatred in his eyes. "You're gonna regret the day you betrayed your family, you little whore."

Blaine slapped his palm into the table hard enough to make his abandoned folder jump an inch. "Don't you fucking *dare* insult my wife!"

My father glared at me, the muscles in his neck working like they always had when he was about to lose his temper. But apparently, being confronted with Blaine's palpable anger made him able to rein it in. Without another word he spun around and stormed out of the office, followed by Michael.

Once the door was closed behind them and we could no longer hear my father shouting profanities and threats as he stomped down the hall, I turned to the still-seething man by my side. My husband.

"You didn't have to do that."

Blaine shot me a dark look. "They harmed you. That's exactly what I needed to do."

Neither Blaine nor I spoke on the car ride home.

I was too wrapped up in the emotional turmoil of what had just happened, and I imagined he was still seething away with anger, at least if the dark look on his face was anything to go by.

When we got home, I went straight up the stairs and threw myself on my bed, burrowing into the duvet. As I lay there, clutching my blankets like a protective shield, my mind went over everything that had been said in that conference room. At first it took all I had not to start crying again, but the more times my thoughts looped, the more they focused on what Blaine had said rather than what my father had. What he'd done.

It was the first time in my entire life anyone had stood up for me. My mother never had the courage nor the strength to do so. She had chosen to accept the abuse instead. I remembered that once I had cried on her shoulder as a little girl over a particularly vicious beating, and she had told me I brought it on myself with my bad behavior.

But not Blaine. He hadn't told me what was done to me was my own fault. And he hadn't seen me as a victim, either.

Somehow, seeing his anger on my behalf and knowing he didn't find me weak and pathetic for what I'd gone through finally gave me the strength to do the same. I had survived years of abuse and come out the other side of it. I was stronger than most people.

I was a survivor.

Tears pooled at the corners of my eyes again, but this time, they were from relief. It felt like a knot in my stomach that had been there so long I'd stopped noticing it finally came undone.

And in some weird, fucked up way, it came undone because of Blaine.

As if summoned by my thoughts, a low knocking on my door announced Blaine's arrival. He walked in without waiting for my answer.

He'd changed out of the suit and back into his usual T-shirt-and-jeans attire, but his face was still set in the same grim lines as when we drove home.

"Hey," I croaked.

"Hey," he said. And then he crossed the room to my bed and climbed in behind me. His arm wrapped around my waist as his body curved around my back, shielding and supporting me.

I closed my eyes and leaned back into his embrace, too emotionally exhausted to protest the unexpected closeness. I didn't care that I wasn't supposed to let him touch me, that our relationship up until now certainly hadn't paved the way for physical closeness like this. All I cared about was that being held by Blaine right now felt better than anything had before.

We lay in silence for a little while, but it was the comfortable kind. The kind that let me feel the press of his muscles against my back, hear his slow breaths in my ear, and smell the faint trace of his cologne without anything disturbing the tranquil enjoyment of the simple, sensory experience of being held this close.

"When I came to see you, I'd just found out my father got my brother locked up on purpose. As punishment. Isaac disobeyed him, refused to kill someone who had snitched on us." Blaine spoke softly, but his mouth was pressed lightly against the side of my head just above my ear, so I heard the pain in his voice perfectly.

"He always taught us that you stick with family, no matter what. Always. Turns out, that doesn't count if you disobey him in any way. He gave his own son over to the *police*, Mira. My *brother*. It's... it's the deepest betrayal. I was so angry. I waited outside my father's house... at night. I had a gun. I..."

I put a hand on the forearm he had wrapped around

my waist, offering him what comfort I could as he fought himself to finally share what had made him desperate enough to seek me out.

"I wanted to kill him," he whispered. "I was going to kill him. I would have, if I hadn't seen Louis and Liam through the window. They were visiting him—I didn't know. I've killed before, but I've never *wanted* to as badly as I did that night. It scared me. It still scares me."

"Do you still want to kill him?" I asked, giving his arm a gentle stroke to ease the roughness in his voice.

He paused for a moment, as if to mull over his answer. "I don't know. I don't think so. But I hate him, Mira. I hate him so much, and it's not meant to be like that. He's my father, and if I don't love him, then I need to at least respect him. Trust his leadership. And I thought I did—until..."

"Until he showed you you can't."

Blaine inhaled deeply, his hot breath tickling my ear. "Yes."

"There comes a time in all our lives when we have to take a step back and decide if the path we're on is one we have freely chosen, or if we are blindly following because it is what is expected of us," I said, twining my fingers with his. His hand was so much bigger than mine, it practically spanned the whole side of my stomach.

Blaine gave my fingers a small squeeze but didn't

move his hand from my grasp. "Is that shrink-Mira speaking, then?"

I smiled at his slightly sardonic tone. "Yeah. It is. My point is, you are experiencing this anger because everything you have been taught was right turned out not to be the One Truth. It's an understandable reaction. You have had your entire foundation pulled from under you. Of course you're angry. And scared. But rather than turn that anger at your father, perhaps it's time to choose your own Truth now. Find your own path."

"I can't do what you did. I can't leave my family. I love my brothers, my crew..." The way he paused made it sound like he'd stopped before finishing the sentence, but he didn't continue.

"You don't have to. But you can choose not to let your father have the same power over you anymore."

He snorted, and I gave his fingers a squeeze to let him know I wasn't done.

"I know how it goes, he's the Big Boss. His word is law. But he can't control your emotions if you don't let him. And—you now see him for what he really is. That gives you a lot of power in how you choose to act on his commands."

He was quiet for a long time, and I thought he wasn't going to say anything else. But just as my eyes started to drift shut, he spoke again.

"You're a pretty smart bird, aren't you?" he hummed

against my ear. His lips brushed against my lobe, raising pleasant goosebumps down the back of my neck.

I chuckled. "Sure. As long as I just need to dispense advice, rather than follow it myself."

"I'm not so sure... I don't know anyone who would have the strength to do what you did, Mira."

Something in his tone made my cheeks warm. It was... admiration, unsoiled by the sarcasm I could have expected from him. When he released my fingers to press his hand against my stomach on top of my scars, my breath turned shaky and my pulse sped up.

Carefully, as if he were trying not to spook a frightened animal, he eased my top up until it rested under my breasts, and raised up on one elbow so he could trace the scars with a fingertip. "Is this why you stopped me? On the stairs? You didn't want me to see?"

I swallowed thickly at the reminder of what had happened between us when he'd chased me up the stairs and pinned me to the floor. He was so close now, and though the gentleness with which he was touching me was in sharp contrast to that night, it was no less effective in making my body hum with mounting desire. I didn't know how to respond, so I just looked at his handsome face as he brushed over my scars, his eyes following the movements of his finger from underneath hooded lids.

"They are battle scars, Mira. Proof of how strong you are. They just make you even more beautiful."

When I didn't answer, he flicked his gaze from my stomach to my face, his gray eyes locking with mine. There was unmistakable heat in them, but it seemed different this time. Less aggressive, even though the intensity still made my stomach flip and my body tingle with awareness.

Slowly, Blaine leaned down toward me. My heart picked up speed again, drumming wildly behind my ribs. Anticipation warred with anxiety over what was happening between us and how everything seemed to have changed in the span of a day. But mostly, I just wanted him to kiss me. Needed him to, though I didn't know why. All I knew was that I might die if he didn't.

He shifted on the bed above and behind me until his lips were inches from mine. I looked up at him, faintly aware that I was breathing heavily, and nearly came undone from the look of pure *need* in his intense gaze.

"Say you want me to," he whispered, and his breath made electricity spark off every nerve in my body.

I reached up and tangled my fingers in his black, tousled hair. It was silky soft and so completely at odds with his hard body hovering above me.

"I do."

Blaine kissed me, his soft lips descending on mine with urgent need.

I clenched my fingers in his hair and kissed him back with a desperation I hadn't known I possessed. It was as if the hollow place in my chest I'd carried around for so many years was ripped wide open, and for every time our frantic lips met, it soothed the waves of loneliness and pain I'd been too scared to face. Until today. With him.

I reached for his belt with an urgency that made him chuckle against my lips. When I got to his zipper it turned to a low groan, and his own hands began grasping for my clothes.

With some maneuvering he managed to pull my top and bra off before I could get any further with his pants. I growled into his mouth with frustration, earning myself a full laugh this time.

Obliging me, Blaine sat up and shrugged out of his T-shirt.

I stared up at all that bare, tattooed skin, drawing in a sharp breath at the sight. Everything about him made me ache with need.

He was lean rather than bulgy, but the strength in his frame was unquestionable. Screw six packs—Blaine had at least a freaking eight-pack, as far as I could count in my less than math-inclined state. I reached out and let my hand slide up across his taut abdomen, enjoying the stacks of hard muscle underneath my fingers. A fine tremor went through his body when I reached the center of his chest and spread my hand out above the place his heart beat. I looked up and was caught off guard by the raw expression in his gray eyes.

"I've never wanted a woman as much as I want you,"

he said, his voice rough. Something in its pitch made my nipples harden and my pulse move down south of my navel.

"Why?" It was the question that had haunted me from that night at the hotel, even if I had done my best to pretend like it didn't. "Why do you want me?"

The corner of Blaine's mouth quirked up, but the heat in his eyes only seemed to flame. "Because you're a fucking goddess." He brushed his hands up my stomach and fanned his fingers out when he came to my chest, pushing my full breasts up in a lewd display. "I love your tits, your round hips, your smart mouth."

"Oh," I croaked, my attention wavering as his thumbs feathered over my already pebbled nipples. He shifted his grip to pinch at both peaks with just the right amount of pressure, and I moaned in response. My body reacted to him like a finely tuned instrument, responding to even his lightest touch. The molten sensation in my pussy made me painfully aware that I was more than ready for him.

"Blaine, I need you inside, now," I said, reaching once again for his belt.

Blaine caught my wrists before I touched the strap of leather, pushing me down flat on my back. "Not yet."

I frowned, frustration seeping in through my lust-filled haze. "Why the hell not?"

He raised an eyebrow at my impatience and gave my wrists a squeeze to ensure I kept them still before he moved to hover above me, his hips resting between my widespread thighs. I arched my pelvis up and he thrust down hard, giving me a sharp jolt of blissful friction right where I needed it.

"*Yes,*" I moaned, attempting to roll my hips up again for more, but he kept my lower body pinned to the mattress.

"Trust me, love," he whispered, letting his hot breath gust over my chest. I groaned with frustration.

"I'll trust you once you're inside of me!"

"Shh," Blaine admonished. And then his lips found mine. His kiss was scorching and left me panting, but he didn't linger. With small nips and hot kisses he trailed up my jawline until he got to my earlobe.

"Every time I see your beautiful body, I want to bend you over and fuck you raw. But if I do that, I miss out on this—on touching every inch of your skin and knowing it makes you ache for it, just as much as I do. I want you to beg for my cock, baby, and I want you to mean it," he murmured into my ear, the brush of his lips against the lobe raising goosebumps with anticipation.

"I mean it *now*. Please, Blaine, *please,*" I breathed shakily. "I've never wanted anything as much as I want this."

His lips curved in a devious smile. "Then imagine how badly you'll want it in about half an hour or so."

"God, you're such a prick," I whined, but without much conviction. Every nerve where his lips had touched me was buzzing with a near-electric awareness, rendering me incapable of gathering my thoughts.

With a hum of amusement Blaine dipped his head to my throat, and I stopped trying to think.

Heat spread in warm waves for every kiss he placed along my jugular, dipping ever lower as he reached my clavicle and lapped at the hollow with his tongue.

I moaned, long and wantonly, clutching at the sheets to keep my hands anchored above my head. As much as I wanted to feel his thick cock force me wide open, I relished in the exquisite torture of his slow caresses.

"Christ, even your skin tastes like sex," Blaine groaned. "Do you have any idea what you do to me?"

Even if I had known what to answer, I wouldn't have been capable, because just then, he moved further down my chest and sucked an achingly erect nipple into his hot mouth.

"Ohh, fuck, *Blaine!*" I moaned, almost losing my grip on the sheets.

He flicked his tongue over the tight little bud and then sucked it deeper into his mouth with short, hard pulls that made me cry out and my clit pulse in sympathy.

When he finally released my nipple with a wet pop, I was panting hard and squirming my hips against his in a desperate attempt at getting more stimulation.

"You have the best fucking tits in the world," he growled—and then he lowered his head to my other breast while simultaneously shifting a leg in between my thighs, lifting it up high enough to rub deliciously against the seam of my jeans.

When he sucked hard on the nipple now trapped in the hot cavern of his mouth, I nearly came.

Nearly—because when I cried out and bucked against his thigh, seconds from reaching my climax, the bastard pulled back, leaving my throbbing body without even the faintest stimulation.

"Blaine!" It was meant as a curse, but it came out breathy and so, so needy.

He fell back down on top of me, but this time, he only gave my breasts a couple of light kisses before he moved further down.

My breath exploded out of my lungs when he trailed his tongue down my soft flesh.

When he got to my scars, he paused, his lips hovering over the very top of them.

I raised up on my elbows to watch him, a small part of me needing to see if he had really meant what he said earlier—about finding them beautiful.

The heat in his eyes when he caught my gaze made me shiver.

"You are the singularly most gorgeous woman on this Earth," Blaine whispered. He bent his head and placed a lingering kiss on the scar highest up on my abdomen.

"So strong."

Another kiss.

"So brave.

Another kiss

"So fucking sexy."

Each touch of his lips against my marred skin trailed lower and lower, not missing a single scar. By the time he reached the waist of my jeans, every drop of blood in my body was on fire.

Blaine sat up, undoing my jeans with skilled speed before he pulled them and my panties over my hips and arse in one go, easily disposing of them in seconds.

When he returned his focus to me, his eyes were smoldering and his lips curved into a smirk that nearly set my panties on fire. "Ready to start begging, love?"

"Yeah-huh," I groaned, desperately hoping I'd be able to form words.

"Good." He moved down further on the bed until he could lay down flat between my legs, his mouth positioned right above my throbbing pussy. His breath blew across my already soaking folds, sending spikes of wild hunger shivering through my body.

The first brush of his tongue over my lips made me whimper and clutch my hands so hard around the sheets that they ripped.

Blaine made an appreciative noise at the back of his throat. "You taste fucking amazing." It was a low growl, and the heady tones went right to my spine.

I arched up, only to be met with the forceful thrust

of the full length of his tongue. He drove in between my lips, parting them from my weeping entrance and all the way up to my pulsing clit in one, long lick.

I cried out, finally losing the battle to keep my hands above my head. When he began lapping circles around my nub of nerves, I grabbed fistfuls of his hair and pulled him as close as I could against me, craving more.

Blaine didn't seem to mind in the slightest. He grabbed my squirming legs and hiked my thighs over his shoulders, before finally closing his lips around my clit to suck deeply.

Once, twice, three times, and I came crashing over the edge, screaming like a banshee.

Every muscle in my body seized to a single, tight knot of hypersensitive flesh, pushed over cliff after cliff by Blaine's persistent suckling on my clit. Only when I collapsed back down on the bed, too weak to move, did he ease up on my pulsing flesh. With a few, gentle kisses he lifted his head to look at me. Despite his smug smirk, the hunger in his eyes was unmistakable.

"Oh my God, Blaine," I gasped. "How did you *do* that? I think... I think I just had an orgasm with my entire body."

"I aim to please," he said, giving me a cheeky wink before he dove back in

"*Ooh!*" My toes curled at the feel of his silky, yet strong laps up the center of my pussy. But what should have been too much so shortly after such a mind-shattering orgasm proved to feel just right. Blaine avoided my clit, kissing, licking and sucking his way up my slick folds until my pleasure-numbed body began to mount once more. I don't know how long he spent reawakening every nerve in my sex, but before he returned his attention to my clit, my hands were once again buried in his hair.

"Come on, Blaine, please," I begged, tugging at his black locks. "Don't tease, please. Oh *God*, I need you."

I swear, I could *feel* his smirk against my lower lips as he ghosted the very tip of his tongue across my aching clit.

"*Yess!*" I hissed, attempting to press my pelvis up against him.

Before I could get anywhere, Blaine released my left leg, letting it flop back down on the mattress so he could shift his grip on me—and once again change his focus from my clit.

I cried out with frustration, but my displeasure cut off when two long fingers slipped into my opening, stretching me deliciously before they curved after my G-spot.

"Oh, yes!" I gasped. *Ohh*, yes, *that* was what I needed! In my desperate desire for Blaine's tongue I had nearly forgotten what I truly craved from him.

Blaine slipped another finger into my tight sheath and began thrusting slowly, making sure he rubbed the soft bit of flesh on my frontal wall.

I bucked and squirmed, lost on pleasure so intense my eyes teared up. But when he finally pressed the flat side of his tongue against my clit, my hands flew up to his forehead, stopping him.

"No, no, not like that. I need you to fuck me, please, oh God, please just fuck me! I want to come on your cock, not your fingers."

Blaine withdrew his fingers before he lifted up, kneeling between my thighs. The look on his face was enough to make my pussy clench.

"I am going to fuck you until you can't take any more," he growled while opening his pants. "I'll give you every inch I've got, and I'm going to make you come on me so hard you won't be able to walk straight, baby."

I swallowed at the sight of his hard cock. Blaine had a lot of inches to give, and though I knew from experience he'd fit, it was impossible not to blanch a little at the prospect of taking all of him.

Blaine trailed a couple of fingers up through my slit, making me shiver with renewed want.

"You're soaking, love," he said, voice as gruff as I'd ever heard it. He leaned forward, supporting his weight on one hand. The other he used to guide his cock to my pussy.

The feel of him against my opening made me draw in a quick breath that turned to a low whimper when he slowly pushed in, spreading me wide on his thick girth.

"Fuck, you feel incredible," he groaned. "So slick and warm."

I was too busy panting and moaning to reply. There was a slight pain from being opened so wide, but mainly, feeling him sliding into the very depths of my being was out-of-this-world amazing. He was gentle with me, in sharp contrast to our first time together, but he never stopped pushing into me until his cock was finally fully hilted. I could feel every single one of his heart beats from where we were connected. I had never been so close with another human being—it felt like our bodies were made for each other, like all I had waited for my entire life was to be one with this man.

I looked up into his eyes and saw a similar expression of revelry painted across Blaine's features.

Then he pulled back, groaning deeply from pleasure, only to thrust back in again the next second. And again. And again.

My world exploded into a wave of sensory ecstasy. The feel of him was so full and so, so good, his thick cock dragging deliciously against my g-spot and filling me past full over and over and over.

I rolled my hips up for more, crying out from being too full, and then did it again—and again, digging my nails into Blaine's strong hips to ensure he didn't pull away.

Not that I'd needed to.

After ensuring I was open enough to take all of him,

Blaine had seemingly had enough of taking it slow. He lifted my thighs over his arms, grabbed my hips tight, and pulled back up for more leverage. And then he fucked me. *Hard.*

I screamed until my throat was sore, thrashing on the bed as I took his cock to the hilt over and over. The wet sounds from my desperately clenching pussy were emphasized by the slapping of flesh as his hips beat against my arse, like an audible proof of just how deep he was going.

It was bliss—the perfect mixture of bone-shattering pleasure from the delicious friction and a full, stretching sort of pain from just how hard I was getting pummeled by Blaine's brutal cock.

I came with a sobbing cry, my pussy clenching down hard on his girth as euphoria made my entire body seize. He fucked me through it, ignoring my pleas for a break until they turned into hard gasps of "*more*" and "*harder.*" Then he complied, pounding into me like a man possessed.

I came again, my orgasm rocketing through my entire body with all the power of an exploding star, and again before I'd ever had a chance to ebb from the first, powerful climax.

On my fourth peak, he came with me.

Blaine groaned deep in his throat, his thrusts turning slightly more erratic until finally, I felt a hot rush of liquid flooding deep inside of me.

He stilled above me, moaning softly as my pussy milked his cock for all he had with tight little spasms while I slowly came down from my own high.

It took several minutes before I was even capable of anything but breathing. But when I looked up at him, warmth spread from my chest to the rest of my already sweaty body.

His eyes were alight with happiness, and the expression in them made my toes curl, despite all my muscles being seemingly out of function. There was so much affection in his gaze it took my breath away. When he bent his head to kiss me, I wrapped my trembling arms around his neck and closed my eyes, certain I'd finally found what I'd been looking for my entire life.

Blaine was gone when I woke up the next morning.

I frowned at the empty side of the bed, where the pillow was still molded where Blaine's head had lain. I touched the sheets experimentally, but they were stone cold. He'd been gone for a while.

My musings came to a quick stop when my stomach lurched, sending me running to the bathroom.

God dammit! Hopefully Rob had gotten me that appointment with a doctor, because I was getting really tired of starting every morning bent over the toilet bowl like this.

When I was finally done, I felt too queasy to worry over why Blaine had left. Probably some sort of business, I thought miserably as I pattered back into my bedroom to get dressed. The world of crime doesn't stop, just because we'd had a heart-to-heart followed by earth shattering sex. I paused mid-way pulling a sleeve over my arm as warmth not related to my upset stomach spread through my chest.

Last night had been... I'd never thought I would be able to open up like that to another person. And I certainly never thought that person could be Blaine.

But he'd not only listened to me, he'd understood—and then he had given me so much in return. He had bared his soul to me.

I was still raw from what the onslaught of emotions yesterday's events had put me through, but it was a good kind of raw in the same way the soreness between my legs felt good. Both were a reminder of Blaine and what we'd shared.

Despite my queasiness, a warm smile spread on my lips. Maybe, just maybe, things would turn out okay. Against all odds and everything we'd thought and everything we'd been through, we might be able to find our happy ever after. Together.

Just as I was about to leave my room, feeling more elated than I had ever been, I caught a glimpse of movement through the window. Moving closer, I peered into the back garden and saw Blaine's tousled, black mane and signature leather coat disappear into the shed.

Huh. Well, at least he was around. Maybe he'd be in for lunch.

I wondered what it'd be like to interact with him now while I headed downstairs to dig into my trusty crackers-and-ginger ale breakfast. Hopefully he wouldn't regret how open he'd been with me. I couldn't face going back to how we used to be. Not now, after what we'd shared last night.

The week's groceries were on the kitchen counter in their usual brown paper bags. Rob might be a crime syndicate's hired muscle, but at least he was eco-conscious.

I plopped down on the bar stool with my box of crackers to sort through the groceries, making sure everything I'd ordered was there. But when my fingers closed around a small, rectangular box, my mind froze in its list-checking tracks with a near-audible screeching.

A pregnancy test.

There was a pregnancy test mixed in with my groceries.

My first thought was that he must have accidentally grabbed it instead of the box of tampons I'd requested. Men and feminine hygiene products, and all that.

I rummaged through the rest of the bags, my fingers frantic enough to rip the paper in the process. It didn't take me long to find the tampons.

Then why...?

Even as I asked myself the possibly quite stupid question, my mind was busy tracking the days since my last period. It was all a bit of a blur, and I'd thought I was due soon—hence the tampon request—but as I went over the calendar days again, I realized I was late. Very late.

My stomach lurched again, this time from absolute terror.

The sickness. The *morning* sickness. My erratic mood swings. The goddamn *pickles*.

With distant amusement I realized Rob had probably witnessed similar behavior in his own wife the two times she'd been pregnant, and had put two and two together. Most of me was busy freaking out, though.

Surely, I couldn't be pregnant. The only man I'd slept with was Blaine, and we... My heart dropped when I remembered last night. We hadn't used any form of protection then, and as far as my fuzzy memory reached, we probably hadn't that night at the hotel either.

Oh, *God*.

Gingerly, I fingered the box. Maybe it was all just coincidental. I mean, I *had* been through an awful lot of stress this past month. It wasn't unreasonable to assume my body was out of whack purely because of that.

At least, there was no reason to freak out until I'd peed on the damn stick.

Twenty minutes—and a pint of ginger ale—later, I sat on the couch in the living room and tapped my fingers against my bouncing leg while I watched the timer on my phone tick down with agonizing sluggishness.

30 seconds until I knew if my life would forever be altered.

Tap, tap, tap, tap, tap, tap.

20 seconds.

What the heck was I gonna *do?* Did Blaine even want a child?

15 seconds.

Did *I* want a child?

10 seconds.

Why couldn't Rob have waited with his sly little shopping surprise until Blaine and I had at least had time to sit down and talk about everything that had happened between us yesterday?

5 seconds.

Oh God, oh God, oh God!

The sharp sound of my phone's timer made me jolt, even though I'd been staring unblinkingly at it for two minutes straight. I snatched it up and flat-out ran to the downstairs bathroom, where I'd left my test.

It lay on the side of the sink, a little blue cross clearly visible even from the door where I was clutching the frame in an effort to keep upright.

I was pregnant.

I was going to have a baby. *We* were going to have a baby.

It was an odd sensation—half of my brain was in the middle of throwing an epic-sized freak-out, complete with violent tremors and hyperventilation. But the other half, the one I clung to in order to not cave to the meltdown and start screaming and/or crying, was completely calm. And happy.

Yes—I wanted a baby. This baby. Blaine's baby.

It wasn't practical, it was the worst possible timing, and I had no idea how Blaine would react, but in the core of my very being I knew without a shadow of a doubt that I wanted this child. With all my heart.

I had to talk to him. Now.

My calm side fused with the freaking out part at that simple thought. I needed to tell Blaine *right now*.

I spun around and was about to run out the front door when I remembered the offensive list he'd made for me on the first day of my arrival. It still hung on the fridge, spelling out the house rules in big, black letters. I wasn't supposed to go into the shed, where I knew he currently was.

No doubt the guys out front knew I wasn't supposed to either, and if I came barging out like the Tasmanian devil then they'd likely stop me from getting to Blaine.

Quickly, I headed toward the window I'd escaped through the night of our big fight. It led into the garden, and I knew it wasn't visible from the front of the house. At night, Blaine had ensured someone was always walking the perimeter after I gave him the slip, but there weren't any men stationed there during the day.

As quietly as I could I clambered through the window and landed in the soft soil underneath. There was a clear line from here to the shed, and with a little luck, no one would spot me before I got there.

I rushed across the dead winter grass and opened the shed without making any sort of noise that could alert Blaine's bodyguards. I felt mighty proud of my own stealthiness as I slipped in through the door.

But before I could open my mouth and call out for Blaine, the scene I'd unwittingly stepped into clicked into place—in crystal clear high-definition. I choked, managing to strangle off a yelp of pure and utter horror.

The shed was fairly big, and immediately in front of me stood a couple of large barrels that half hid me from view. Perhaps that was why Blaine didn't see me. Or perhaps it was because he was completely focused on the man he had tied up on a chair in the middle of the shed. There was plastic wrapping spread out underneath him and splatters of blood covered it. His body was covered in bruises and lacerations.

Blaine swung his arm, and the chain in his hand whipped through the air and cut deeply into the man's flesh. He screamed, but a gag in his mouth cut off the sound so only a whimper escaped.

The world seem to spin. My knees gave in and I halfway fell into a crouch behind the barrels, breathing deeply to not make a sound, even though my chest was tight with horror and grief.

I'd seen this scene before. Too many times to count. My brothers, my father, and their men had done this in our basement. To enemies, snitches, and people who failed to pay up.

Torture.

Blaine was torturing that man.

Metal instruments and ropes on the wall spoke their clear language of what this place was. This shed in my backyard. It was a torture chamber.

I had run away from my family to get away from a world where rooms like this were a part of life.

Another whack of metal against flesh rung through the shed and was followed by another, muted whimper.

I don't know why I had allowed myself to forget what he was.

As open as he had been with me last night, it didn't change the fact that he was dangerous to the core. There might be more than ruthless violence within him. I'd seen it last night. But this... this was everything I'd feared my whole life, everything I'd fought to escape.

As quietly as I could, I crept back out of the shed and back to the window. It took a bit of climbing, but I made it back into the house.

My stomach roiled, and I made my way to the bathroom to throw up again. I wasn't sure if it was from the pregnancy or the violence I'd witnessed.

The pregnancy. *The baby.*

I pressed a hand to my stomach as I curled up next to the toilet while my dry heaves calmed down.

No. I couldn't bring a baby into this kind of world. I

couldn't doom an innocent life to live through what I had had to.

Which meant... which meant I had to save it. I had to go somewhere where the child growing inside of me would never be subjected to the violence in a family like the Steels.

Sorrow warred with determination as I walked up the stairs to pack the few necessities I could fit in my hand bag. When I was done, I found pen and paper and sat down to write a note.

Whatever else Blaine was, the moment between us last night had been real. And the emotions in my heart that had finally been let out while we made love were real too.

Perhaps it was for the best. If I stayed, I would never be able to get free from this world, because he would be there—pulling me back in. And if I didn't get out now, I would soon be powerless to resist.

It's funny how things become so crystal clear when we're about to lose them. As I climbed back out of the window and found my way over the tall fence surrounding the garden, I knew I was leaving behind my one true chance at love.

But I knew all that mattered now was to protect the innocent life in my womb.

Even if it was from its own father.

. . .

BLAINE,

I'm so sorry.

I can't do this. I can't be your pretend wife—I can't live a life filled with violence.

I have left London and I will never be back. Please, if you ever felt anything for me, if what we shared last night was real, then don't come after me.

Let me be free.

Mira.

TWENTY-ONE
4 MONTHS LATER
MIRA

The smell of orange blossoms and sea swept over my face as I made my way through the narrow streets of Barcelona's Casco Viejo. I'd rented a small flat above a butcher shop not far from the café where I worked most days, brewing coffee and serving tables.

As every time I made my way home, I was thankful it was only a short walk. My ankles were always terribly swollen after a day on my feet, and my lower back ached something fierce. The shouts and hollers from the people filling the streets marking the beginning of the evening's social events only made me yearn for my bed all the more.

Sighing with relief, I let myself into the stairway that led to my tiny apartment and climbed the steps with a hand pressed against my swollen belly. Every time I stepped foot on stairs the baby within would begin to kick up a storm, and the only thing that could stop it from demolishing my bladder was apparently the light press of a hand.

"Just as difficult as your father," I muttered while attempting to unlock my front door with the same hand that held the bit of shopping I'd done on my way home.

Blaine. I bit my lip to stem the onslaught of mixed emotions the thought of him always brought on.

He had been looking for me since the day I ran away. I'd thought he would either stop caring once it was obvious I'd left the country, or he would have respected my plea in the letter to let me go. I'd been very wrong.

My advanced pregnancy didn't make the stress of having to pack up and leave every four weeks or so any easier to deal with, but of course, he didn't know I was pregnant. I'd made sure to take all traces of the pregnancy test with me when I left so he would never know his runaway wife was with child.

I gave into the urge to flop down on my bed for a few moments before I had to start dinner. I was exhausted every minute of every day, and all I wanted to do after a long day's work was to go to sleep—but the baby had other ideas. Getting by on whatever service job I could find wasn't made any easier by my constant hunger. "Eating for two"—yeah, right. I scoffed and rubbed my belly as the baby moved restlessly within. If my pregnancy appetite was anything to go by, I was expecting at least quintuplets.

I ate my dinner in front of the open French door overlooking the bustling street below. Then I went to sleep on my narrow single bed before the nightclub a few roads over got too loud.

***

"HELLO, LITTLE CUNT."

The menacing snarl ripped me out of my uneasy slumber with a start. My heart kicked into overdrive the second my eyes flew open, but it was much too late to react.

Someone pressed a cold, sharp edge to my throat and grabbed hold of my hair before I could even orientate myself.

I cried out from the sharp pain in my scalp, but quieted down instantly when the knife against my throat pressed in in warning.

He had found me.

"Please, Blaine, you're hurting me," I croaked. Even in my panicked state, even after I'd fled from him for four months after seeing him viciously torture a bound and helpless man, some part of my brain didn't believe he would physically harm me. I reached up to put my hand against his to try to calm him—even if he didn't mean me harm, the knife was a pretty vivid indication that he was furious.

The tug on my scalp instantly eased as he let go of my hair.

"Look, I know you're mad at me—" I didn't get to continue before, out of nowhere, the backside of a hand impacted with my cheek so hard I saw stars. The blow was forceful enough to throw me back down on the mattress.

"Blaine!" I cried, cradling my cheek. I don't know what was more painful—the smack, or the shattering of what I dimly realized was the last of my crushed belief in there being any goodness in the man my stupid heart had fallen for.

"*Blaine.* You think crying out for your husband will save you, you dumb cow?"

I froze stiff on the bed, my tears drying from sheer horror. I knew that voice. And it didn't belong to Blaine.

The naked light bulb that was the sole source of light in my rented accommodation flickered on, and I was greeted with the very image that had haunted my nightmares since I was eighteen years old.

Above me, next to the bed, my brother Michael crouched down. He was holding a sharp blade in one hand, pointing it at me in an unspoken threat. Behind him I could see my father, his arms crossed over his stocky chest and his mouth pressed into a thin line, and over by the light switch stood my other brother

Devlen. A gun stuck up from the waistband of his jeans.

I stared at them in abject terror, my mind threatening to slip into the blank space it had when they found me in London, just to get away.

"Oho, would you look at that!" Michael hooted. He pointed at my stomach with his knife. "Either she's gotten fatter than ever, or Steel put a bastard in her whore cunt before she gave him the slip."

My father moved closer and I cringed back against the wall, my hands automatically flying up to protect my belly.

"Well, well, well. No wonder Blaine's been searching for you so desperately for the past four months, huh, Aignéis? And here I thought we might just get the pleasure of blackmailing the Steels for a couple of million while showing all of London how easy it is to humiliate the so-called greatest crime syndicate in the city. Turns out our prize sow's got a little surprise for us." He knelt down next to the bed and gave me a cold smile. "What do you think the Steels will give up in return for the safe return of an heir to the empire? The entire city?"

I shook my head and pressed my hands harder against my stomach. As much as I wanted to flee into sweet oblivion, I couldn't—not when it would leave my unborn child at their mercy. "They don't know about the baby. They won't believe you."

"I guess we'll just see about that." Quick as a snake, he twisted around and grabbed my hands so he could pull them up above my head and away from my belly.

I screamed and bucked, doing everything I could to get free, but Michael rolled up onto my legs so he could pin them against the mattress with all his weight. My father stuffed a cloth in my mouth, cutting off my screams for help.

"There we go. Get her top off—we want to show Daddy what we've got to offer in return."

Michael gave me a lecherous smirk before he lowered the knife to my stomach. I whimpered in fear and tried to squirm, but all I managed to do was pull the muscles in my arms.

Slowly, letting me feel the tip of the blade against my skin as he cut, Michael slid the knife up along the middle of my camisole, letting my stomach and breasts spill out.

"Devlen, take the pictures," my father said.

My brother moved across the room and pulled out his phone.

"Make sure you get her face and stomach."

"And the knife," Michael added, letting the blade slide down along the scars on my stomach. "Just so he gets the idea."

"I told you you'd regret the day you betrayed your family," my father growled into my ear while Devlen's phone flashed, snapping picture after picture of my exposed and pinned-down body. "And if your beloved husband doesn't come through, you're going to regret ever leaving the Steels' protection. I'll cut that baby from your belly with a steak knife if he doesn't hand over control of London's underworld. So what do you think, Aignéis? Does he love you and your baby more than he does the Family?"

"We're pretty sure she's in Spain now, but where exactly we don't know yet. Sorry, boss."

I gritted my teeth and pressed "end" on the call, clenching my fist so tight around the phone the casing protested.

Four months. It had been four months since I came home to an empty house and a note that damn near tore my guts out, and I was no closer to finding Mira than I had been then.

Let me be free, she'd written. Perhaps if she had left me before I bared my soul to her, before I realized that she was the one person in this damn world that could ever make me feel whole, I could have let her go. I would have at least tried to. But not now—not when I'd finally tasted what true happiness was like. I couldn't give that up again—I couldn't give *her* up without destroying myself.

I had hunted for her myself those first two weeks, until Louis and Liam found me in Berlin.

That's when I learned how my father viewed the *"embarrassing situation"*—as he called it.

The twins told me that he'd ordered me to return home immediately and not waste any more resources on chasing down my *"floozy of a wife."* That he was furious with me for letting her escape and humiliate the family, and wanted me to cut all ties to her.

The only thing that kept me from disowning him then and there was Liam's and Louis' hasty promise that they would continue the search, and their reminder that I'd be no good to anyone, let alone her, if I disobeyed our father's orders and ended up in America as a result. Or in prison.

Since then, each of my brothers had spent a week here and a few days there traveling around Europe under the guise of business arrangements. Even Marcus came to my aid, without ever being asked.

Currently, I had one of my men searching Southern France, the last known place she'd been. He would have to come home soon, though, to avoid rousing my father's suspicion.

I cursed into the darkness of my room. Every time I had to pull a man home and replace him with another, it pushed back the search by several days, which was plenty of time for vital trails to go cold. Because of my own father, my wife was out there somewhere, alone and probably scared.

My heart spasmed. I knew why she'd run.

I saw the long, red hair snagged on the door to the shed while I searched the property for clues as to where she'd gone. She'd seen me interrogate the guy I'd snuck out of bed after our night together to find.

If she was scared, she was scared of *me*.

But when I found her, I would explain. I would make her understand, and she would see why I had to do what I did. She *had* to.

A beep from my phone pulled my swirling thoughts from the void they'd been circling. I looked down and saw the little email icon in the top right corner.

Probably Lester sending me written details of Mira's possible whereabouts.

I swiped my thumb over the display to open the mail —and nearly dropped it on the floor.

What flashed up on my email were not simple instructions. It was a photo. Of Mira.

My heart skipped a beat. Two beats. Three. Then, with a burst of pain and sickening fear, it began beating again, pounding in overdrive behind my ribs as if it was trying to burst free.

Someone held down her arms above her head, but the photo cut off just above her terrified eyes. I did recognize the guy holding a knife to her scarred stomach, though. It was her brother—the one who'd come to my office.

I stared at her swollen belly until my retinas burned from the pain of my phone's sharp backlight.

She was pregnant.

She was carrying my child.

And her sick family had them both.

"I DON'T *CARE* if he's sleeping!" I punched my fist so hard against the door frame, the pictures lining the hallway wall in my father's home shook. Sharp pain in my knuckles made my hand spasm, but I was too angry to pay it any mind.

Wesley flinched—a look that would have been amusing on the nearly seven feet tall and four feet wide body guard if I'd been able to feel anything but rage and desperation just then.

"You know he'll be pissed, Blaine," he tried to reason with me. "He's made his feelings about your wife known. I'm just trying to save you from yourself, here."

"I swear, if you don't go get him *right fucking now,* I'm going to kick in your goddamn teeth," I hissed.

Something in my face must have shown how serious I was, because Wesley finally held up his hands in surrender and sighed. "Fine. I tried. Go sit in the drawing room. I'll wake him."

I spent the next fifteen minutes pacing back and forth in front of the unlit fireplace, periodically glancing at the email. As much as it hurt to the core of my soul to see my wife so scared and vulnerable, her image was the only thing that kept me grounded enough to not start smashing furniture. I needed to keep a level head for her. And for our baby.

When my father finally came into the parlor, he was wearing a silk bathrobe and a sour expression.

"What is this, Blaine? Wesley says you threatened him in order to get me up? If this is about that goddamn wife of yours, I swear—"

"It's about my goddamn wife and your grandchild," I hissed, shoving my phone up underneath his nose. "She's pregnant, Dad. And the Clerys have her. They're threatening to—" it took everything I had to finish that sentence "—to butcher her. And my *child*."

I watched my father's eyebrows raise a quarter of an inch as he took in the image.

"This is why I told you to stop raising hell. You've made it abundantly clear that she means a lot to you, with how you tore through half of Europe before I dragged you back here. Of course she was going to get herself kidnapped. And what do the Clerys want, then? Money?" He sounded exasperated.

His tone made me bristle. "*She* didn't do this. *They* did."

"Indeed, they did. And maybe if you hadn't cut all

our business ties with them and threatened to '*gut them like fish*,' they wouldn't have bothered hunting the little tramp down to get back at you. Now, what do they want?" My father folded his arms across his chest and leveled me with one of his trademark no-nonsense stares.

I swiped my thumb over my phone, scrolling further down in the email to the short message the Clerys had included. "They want control over London. Over all of it."

My father snorted and unfolded his arms. "Ah, the Clerys—you have to love their gumption. They always did have more balls than they did brains. Tell them they can have three hundred thousand pounds and that's it. If they're not happy with it, they can start cutting slices off the lass and see how far that will get them."

"I am not telling them that," I seethed. "I'm not risking her life."

He shrugged, turning toward the door. "That's all I'm prepared to offer, and that's only because I recognize my part in this. If I hadn't made you marry the girl, this whole spectacle could have been avoided. Though I am surprised and disappointed in your lapse of judgment, Blaine. All of this for a wife you didn't want? She must have quite the magical snatch."

"That's your grandchild's life you're throwing away," I said, only barely maintaining my composure. "You know they will follow through on their threats if they don't get what they want. You might not care about my wife, but that baby is your *blood*. '*Everything for the Family*,' remember? That *used* to be our motto."

"Oh, please." He turned fully to the door and stepped toward it, clearly not intending on continuing the conversation any further. "She's been gone how long? More than likely, that kid belongs to the first piece of Euro trash she bedded in exchange for a meal. Don't be so sentimental, Blaine. It's not doing you nor the Family any good."

"Don't you dare walk away from me!"

My roar made my father stop halfway out the door. He looked at me over his shoulder, the expression of cold contempt clear in his gray eyes. "*Watch it*, son. I have tolerated your foolishness so far. It will not continue much longer. Do not presume my acknowledgment of my part in introducing you to this girl will extend to any further attempts at returning her. I suggest you think carefully before you speak again."

I clutched my hands into fists by my sides, once again nearly breaking my phone. "Or what, you'll send me to jail like you did Isaac?"

His back stiffened, a look of surprise filtering across his face before he managed to squash it. Slowly, he turned back to me.

"Yeah, I know what you did. I know you were the one to get Isaac locked up for crossing you. And if you try to stop me from saving Mira, I swear to God, I will let all of them know. Isaac, Jeremy, Liam, Louis, Marcus and every single one of our men will know that you betrayed your own family for petty revenge."

"You have no idea what you're talking about." My father tried to regain his usual, cold composure, but it was clear my knowledge of his deceit had startled him.

"I know that if it gets out, you've lost them. All of them. And what will your empire be then? Will you be able to keep hold of your precious power if all your sons turn their backs on you? I doubt it. I doubt it very much."

I hadn't planned on confronting him with what I knew. Ever. I knew the second I opened my mouth and shared what I'd learned, he would see me as an enemy—and William Steel was not a man you wanted as an enemy. But his arrogant dismissal of my plea for help and his complete indifference to my wife and my child made me realize that he already *was* my enemy.

Anyone who would stop me from coming to Mira's aid was an enemy. And one thing I'd learned from him was you crushed your opposition before they could ever get a chance of hurting you.

"You don't want to give up your power to save your son's wife and your own grandchild? Fine. But you *will* help me save them, Father, or your dirty little secret won't be a secret anymore."

TWENTY-THREE

MIRA

The warehouse was cold enough to make me shiver in my T-shirt and shorts, but it was still a relief from the past three days. I'd been zip-tied and locked in the back of a van while my family made the drive up through Europe, so the open space above my head felt like a blessing.

I tried to ignore how the zip-ties around my wrists and ankles dug into my flesh while I drank in big gulps of the cool, fresh air. If this was going to be my last night on this Earth, then I wanted to at least have one moment's pleasure, however faint and fleeting.

"Who would have thought little Aignéis would be able to bring the infamous Steel family to its knees? If I were Blaine, I'd let us cut that little bastard out of your belly before I'd give up London."

I shuddered as my moment's peace was shattered by

Michael's cold, disparaging voice, and looked up to see him carelessly flick his knife back and forth between his fingers as he leaned against the pallets nearest to where I sat tied to a chair. My dad had ordered him to watch over me while he and Devlen set up their men around the perimeters, to make sure they were prepared in case the Steels were planning an ambush. My father's orders were clear—if anything was amiss, Michael was to plunge the knife first into my belly, and then into my heart. He had given him the orders right in front of me, undoubtedly because he wanted to relish the sick wave of fear his words inspired.

"Guess they really are as soft as the rumor claims, when it comes to women and family."

I closed my eyes to not have to look at Michael. If there truly were such rumors about the Steels, then I knew they were as false as false could be. And that's why I knew I was going to die tonight.

Even if Blaine somehow got the noble inclination to give up his family's empire for me and our baby, I knew there was no chance on this Earth that his father would comply. The man who had sent his own son to jail for disobeying his orders would not give up an ounce of power for Blaine's unwanted wife and child.

And without William Steel, there was no deal.

If Blaine hoped to overpower them with a large group of his men, I would be dead before he ever got to me.

I bit my lip hard to stop the tears from flowing again. I'd cried and pleaded enough the past three days—I didn't want to waste my last hours with more. It was too late for regrets now—too late to think about what would have happened if I'd stayed with Blaine.

I only wished my hands were free so I could feel my baby move underneath my palms one last time.

"There's a car coming."

I opened my eyes at the scratching noise from the walkie in Michael's belt and my heart sped up. This was it.

"Any red flags?" my brother asked into the walkie.

"Not so far. Looks like there's just Blaine on his own. We'll be in in about half a minute, stay sharp."

Michael sent me a wide smile that didn't reach his eyes. "Did you hear that, sis? Looks like Daddy's coming to save you all on his own. How *romantic.*"

I stared at him. When we were little, we'd played together almost every day. Devlen had never been interested, but Michael and I had been close. It all ended the day my dad caught him playing with dolls with me and gave him the worst beating of his life for playing with *"girl toys."* He hardly spoke to me in the years that followed, not until that night he and Devlen held me down so my father could carve his fury into my stomach.

Maybe after a few more decades I could have come to pity him for what my father did to twist his spirit so horrifically, but not now. Not after he had held his knife to my stomach and threatened my unborn child.

Now, all I felt for him was hatred.

The walkie buzzed again, drawing both of our attention. *"We're coming in."*

"Showtime," Michael said with a wink in my direction. He moved behind me, and I felt the cold steel of his blade press up against my throat. Then the doors to the warehouse slid open with a metallic clang, revealing three figures against the backdrop of the darkness outside. The figure in the middle carrying a briefcase towered over the two men flanking him.

Blaine.

They walked through the door, and finally, I could see his face. He was as handsome as ever, but behind the calm mask he'd schooled his features into, I could see something else in his eyes: dark, dangerous and all-consuming rage.

I swallowed thickly as he stared at me, suddenly more anxious about the man standing in front of me than the one who had a knife to my throat. Blaine was *pissed,* and I had a feeling it wasn't just with the men who had tried to blackmail him.

"That's far enough," Michael hissed from behind me when Blaine didn't stop where Devlin indicated. He pressed the knife tighter against my skin, and I grimaced when I felt the blade bite in.

Blaine stopped, his eyes sweeping over my disheveled figure.

"You've mistreated my wife." His voice was as calm as his face, but there was an unmistakable threat lurking beneath the surface.

"The little bitch struggled," my father said calmly as he sauntered up next to Blaine. "And this ain't the Ritz. What have you got in the briefcase, kid? Something that will make this go down the easy way, I hope."

Finally, Blaine took his gaze off me and leveled it at my father. "This is every deed to every business, estate and asset my family owns, along with the key to every one of our bank deposit boxes. There's also a small upfront payment of £200,000, as you requested. Upon the safe return of Mira and myself, my father will call a meeting with the other heads of London's underworld and let them know you now own our empire."

"And what guarantee do I have the old man will keep his word?" Despite his attempt at sounding tough, my father couldn't keep his eyes off the briefcase. His excitement was nearly palpable, even across the room.

Blaine arched an eyebrow at him. "I do believe handing over the deeds to everything we own is a reasonable insurance. But if you insist, please do go through the paperwork. I can wait."

My father practically snatched the briefcase out of Blaine's hands and ripped it open. I couldn't see the contents, but from the look on my father's face, it was everything Blaine had said it was.

I frowned with confusion. How the hell had Blaine convinced his father to do this?

And *why?*

He looked at me again then, and my heart gave an achy spasm in my chest at the change in his stormy eyes.

There was still anger in them, yes, but behind there was so much more. Devotion. Need.

Love.

I stared at him, faintly aware my mouth was hanging open as my brain finally processed what my heart had hoped for in the most shameful, most secret parts of my soul.

It was love that had made my husband come to this dark warehouse to get me—love that had made him give in to blackmail, and love that had made him somehow do the impossible and get his father to give up his empire. I still had no idea how he had done it, but the why was so painfully clear on his beautiful face as he watched me from across the concrete floor.

He loved me.

The tears came then, and there was nothing I could do to stop them.

All my life I had ached to know that somewhere out there, there was one person who would give me what I'd never had while growing up.

My mother had loved me, to some extent, but not so

much that she lifted a finger to spare me from my father's brutality.

Never in a million years would I have thought I would experience that from the man who had resented me since the day we met. The man I had run away from and taken his baby with me.

"Please cut my wife free. You don't need her as a bargaining chip anymore." Blaine's voice was as calm as ever, only hinting at slight disdain. When I managed to blink the tears away and look into his eyes again, the swirl of emotions was gone, hidden behind the mask once more.

"Do as he says," my father grunted without looking up from the briefcase. "He's unarmed anyway—they're not going anywhere before we're done."

The knife finally moved from my throat, and cut through the zip-ties holding my hands together behind my back.

I bit down on a cry when blood came rushing to my fingers, aggravating the place on both my wrists where the tie had dug in deep.

Michael repeated the process with first one, and then the other of my ankles and then proceeded to get me out of the chair with a hard shove against my spine.

I stumbled forward, unable to keep my balance while my feet were still numb from the lack of circulation, but before I smacked face-first into the concrete, strong arms closed around me, breaking my fall.

Blaine lifted me up on my reluctant feet, supporting my body against his own. The heat from him enveloped me like a cocoon, but it was the unwavering strength of his arms as he held me that made a wave of overpowering relief wash over me, premature as it may be.

We might still be unarmed and at the mercy of my family, but I wasn't alone anymore—Blaine was here. Somehow, someway, he would see us safely out of this.

"You okay?" he asked, his voice gruff, but the tone was completely contradicted by how gently he placed a hand on my rounded belly. "Both of you?"

"I think so," I croaked. "Blaine, I—"

Blaine lifted the hand from my stomach to brush his finger against my lips, silencing me. "Shh, love. We'll talk when we're home."

Right, okay. Talking through all our intimate baggage would have to wait until we were not surrounded by enemies. I guess I could wait—not in the least because the longer we waited, the longer it would be until I would have to drag myself out of the fairytale where the man who loved me had come to save me and everything would turn out alright. The harsh reality where I had run away from him because I had seen him torture another man could wait.

I pressed my hand tightly against my stomach and leaned in against Blaine. He had come for me, and he would see me safely out of the danger. For now, that was all that mattered.

Blaine held me tightly against his side while we both watched my father and Devlen go through all the papers in the briefcase in silence. It wasn't until Michael looked away from us to play with his knife, clearly bored by waiting around without getting to threaten anyone, that I realized Blaine was doing much more than waiting.

The hand he hadn't wrapped around my shoulders dug into the pocket of his leather jacket for a moment. I could see the rectangular outline of a phone against the leather and bit down on a small gasp.

He hadn't simply surrendered to my family, and whatever plan was about to unfold, he'd just set it in motion.

My heart thumped unevenly in my chest. What if he didn't know my family had a good dozen or so of their men circling the perimeter? If his men tried to storm the warehouse, they would get taken down before they could ever get to us. And we would both be executed.

My fear must have shown on my face, because Blaine lifted his hand back up to my face and cupped my cheek.

"It'll be alright, I promise," he mumbled.

I stared into his eyes, searching for the confirmation that he knew exactly what he was doing. I found it when his mouth hitched up in a smirk.

Even in as fucked up a situation as this, Blaine Steel was still the self-assured man I'd met so many months ago.

"Boss, there's trouble coming. A fuck-ton of police is driving up. Do we shoot?"

The unexpected sound from my father's walkie made everyone inside the warehouse freeze mid-movement.

I stared at Blaine, mouth open. The police? The one rule everyone in the underworld never, *ever* broke was to never involve the police. You did that and your reputation was done for. For good.

There would not be a criminal in the country who didn't view him as a traitor. Him, and his entire family.

"You didn't!" my father hissed. He spun around from the briefcase to face Blaine. "You fucking snitch!"

"Yeah. I did." Blaine released his hold on me to fold both arms across his chest as he took a step forward. "Or rather, one of my brothers did. I believe he might have mentioned a big drug deal gone wrong and a pregnant hostage being caught in the middle—something like that. You know how nostalgic those coppers get as soon as you aim a gun at a pregnant woman. So go ahead, tell your men to start shooting at the police. I'm sure that'll end well for you."

"Boss?" The frantic-sounding man on the other end of the walkie said. *"I need orders. They're almost on us."*

"For fuck's sake, stand down, you idiot!" my father hissed into the walkie before he tossed it aside. *"Fuck!"*

"You should never have crossed my Family," Blaine said, his tone as cold as the ice in his eyes.

My father grabbed Devlen's gun out of his hand. Wild with rage, he pointed it right at Blaine's chest. "*You* should have kept your mouth shut, boy. I will *not* be disrespected. You think your name protects you? When it gets out what you've done here today, you're through. Your entire family will be dead before summer, including her. And *you* won't be there to stop it."

"You're not going to kill me," Blaine said, not so much as flinching as he stared the barrel of the gun down. "If you shoot me now, you'll go down for murder as well as everything else, and you don't have enough time to make anyone take the fall for you before the police get here. Yeah, I know how you operate, Clery. You're a coward, deep down. That's why you need to abuse those who are too weak to defend themselves. You don't have the fucking balls."

My heart dropped and adrenaline and fear roared through my veins when I saw the rage in my father's eyes snap.

Blaine was right—my father was a coward, who would only strike when he was sure to win. But he had made one fatal miscalculation—because the only thing my father truly cared about was receiving the respect he thought belonged to him.

I knew he was going to pull the trigger before Blaine had finished his insult.

"No!" I didn't have time to think—only to react. I

threw myself in front of Blaine just as my father's finger pulled back, shoving him out of the way.

Pain lanced through me, emphasizing the sound of the gun being fired. I screamed and crumpled to the floor, clutching my side. It felt like my flesh had melted into pure, liquid pain. My vision blackened and blurred. Then my head hit the concrete with a muffled thud.

"Mira! No!"

The last thing I heard was Blaine's roar of anguish. Then everything went dark.

Slow, monotonous beeping pulled me from the depths of nothingness.

Groggily, I opened my eyes. Bright, fluorescent light and the smell of antiseptics made me grimace and shield my eyes, but when I lifted a hand to cover my face a pang of dull pain from my side made me gasp.

"Doc says it's just a nasty flesh wound. You and the wee one will both be fine."

I slowly lowered my hand from my face to peer in the direction of the speaker. He was sitting in a chair next to my bed, his flaming red hair brightening up the otherwise sterile hospital room.

"Liam?"

"Louis," he corrected me, a wicked smile curving the corner of his mouth. "Liam went home with a nurse a few hours ago, left me to the incredibly boring job of waiting for you to wake up on my own. No offense."

"Sure," I said, frowning with confusion. "But why? Where's Blaine?" My heart dropped as I remembered the gunshot. Had I not managed to push him out of the line of fire after all? Oh God, *no.* "Louis, *where is he?*"

"Calm down, he's fine. Got held up at the police station after bashing Clery's head in. Our dad's working on getting him out. Until then, Liam and I have been tasked with keeping you safe and sound." The redhead stretched lazily. "So far, it's been a supremely tedious task. How long until you think you can manage a half-arsed escape attempt?"

"What do you mean, *'bashing Clery's head in'?*" I asked, ignoring his playful dig. Waking up after getting shot and finding out the man who rescued you has been arrested doesn't lend itself to playful banter. "Did he *kill* someone?"

"Nah, the police got there in time. Your dad's... well, he's not fine, but I guess he's gonna live. Sadly." Louis gave me a somewhat apologetic look. "Sorry."

As if I cared if my monster of a father lived or not. The only reason I felt a stab of relief was that I didn't want Blaine to get charged with murder. I doubted even Steel connections could have gotten him out of that one.

"So what happens now?" I looked at Blaine's brother with some hesitation. He didn't *seem* upset that I'd run away and effectively damaged the Steel's reputation, but I doubted I was in anyone's good graces.

Louis shrugged. "Once you get discharged, you're coming home with Liam and me until Blaine gets out. Marcus offered to look after you, but lucky for you, Blaine refused. And after that—well, I guess it's up to whatever you and Blaine work out. I wouldn't expect another vacation to the Mediterranean anytime soon, though. My brother was ever so upset after you gave him the slip, and that was before he knew about the baby."

I took in a deep breath and let it seep out slowly, taking some of my leftover anxiety with it. If Blaine's brother was this relaxed about the whole thing, then perhaps the rest of the family was too.

"And the Family? Blaine ratted my— the Clerys out to the police. I know how big of a deal that is."

Louis winced, somewhat ruining my beginning sense of calm. "You really don't need to worry about that, Mira."

"It's kind of hard not to," I said, my voice more than a little dry. "Seeing as this all happened because of me."

"Nah, sweets, it happened because of the Clerys. You didn't ask to get kidnapped, did you?" He offered me an easy smile. "And no one gets to hurt a Steel and walk away. Whatever it takes, we protect our own. No matter if my idiot brother gets things ironed out with you or not, you're a Steel now."

I WAS DISCHARGED the next day. Though I was still sore, I was able to move around okay, as long as I took things slow.

The twins turned out to be decent hosts. They set me up in Liam's bedroom with fresh linen and my bottles of medicine and vitamins laid out on the night stand. When I asked where Liam would sleep, feeling bad about putting him out of his bedroom, I got a cheeky wink and a "Don't you worry about that, sweetheart," as response. I figured it involved the pretty nurse he'd picked up while hanging around my hospital room and didn't ask any more questions.

Marcus showed up a few hours after the twins took me home. He let himself into the flat and sat down in an armchair close by the door—and proceeded to not speak a word to me nor the twins.

When I got up the next morning, he was still there, staring straight ahead into the turned-off flat screen TV that decorated most of the near wall. The twins' flat was a bachelor pad through and through.

"Just ignore him," Louis—at least, I thought it was Louis—yawned as he came around the corner from the hallway and saw me looking at his brother. "If he doesn't want to speak, it's best to just leave him alone."

I frowned in confusion and followed Louis—still

wasn't completely sure, the twins were impossible to tell apart as far as I could see—to the kitchen.

"Why is he here?"

"Dunno," he shrugged. "Possibly thinks we can't look after a pregnant lady, or he's making sure you don't escape. Or he's just in the mood for company. He's my brother and I'd die for him, but he's nuts as fuck. To tell you the truth, back when he called Blaine and said you were at his place, we were all a bit concerned he'd done something to you. Eggs?"

I blinked at his nonchalant tone. "Er... sure. Thanks." I sat down at the small cafe table in the corner by the window overlooking the river while the twin began to cook breakfast. "He was quite nice to me, actually."

"Marcus? Huh. That's a first."

"That's not very nice, Louis," I chided, feeling a bit protective of the man who had shown me kindness when I'd needed it the most.

"Liam. And maybe not, but it's true. There's a reason Blaine noped right out of having you stay with him. Again, he's my brother, but if I had a pregnant wife I wouldn't let him within fifty yards of her, either. You think Blaine's bad? He's a fucking puppy dog in comparison."

Huh. "What happened to the nurse?"

"Louis is with her—it's his turn." Liam poured two

mugs of tea and brought one over to me, before he returned to the frying pan as if he hadn't said anything out of the norm. A promising scent of bacon was beginning to spread in the kitchen.

"His *turn?* And she's okay with that?" I regretted asking the second the words left my mouth, and flushed hotly.

The redhead flashed me a wicked grin. "Who says she knows? We're identical, after all."

"That's..." Exactly the sort of shit I could imagine guys like the Steel brothers getting up to. I shook my head and cradled the hot mug. It wasn't my concern—I had enough to deal with right now, without trying to school Blaine's brothers on how to treat women. "Never mind."

Liam winked at me, but thankfully didn't comment further.

***

BLAINE GOT out later that afternoon.

Louis—who'd come back sometime during the late morning—poked his head into Liam's bedroom just past two to let me know he was on his way to get me.

I spent the next forty-five minutes quietly freaking out.

I had no way of knowing how this would go down—

how *he* would react to seeing me, now that there was no immediate danger. I was positive what I'd seen in his eyes in that warehouse was love, and for him to risk his life *and* the entire Steel empire to get me, there had to be more than hurt pride in it. But I was under no illusion that Blaine Steel was happy with me. There had been pure fury in his eyes too, and I was pretty certain it wasn't all reserved for my father.

I had left him, after we'd bared our souls to each other. I'd run away with his child.

Whatever he may feel for me, I wasn't sure it would be a positive outcome for me.

And then there were my own messed up emotions.

I had wanted him from the very start. I'd thought it was pure, physical attraction, because I'd been too scared to even consider the alternative. And then, when he'd finally let me in... I had been so overwhelmed with everything, so wrapped up in the way he made me feel safe and protected. The way my entire being sang for him.

The next time I'd seen him, he had been brutally torturing a man.

Even now, the thought of seeing the man I'd let myself be vulnerable with be so savage made my heart flutter with fear. If he was capable of such violence, would I ever truly be safe with him? Would my child?

As if the baby knew I was thinking about its father,

it moved restlessly inside. I put a hand against my stomach to soothe it.

I wanted to be with him more than I had ever wanted anything else. No one had ever made me feel like he had. But I couldn't let my own feelings come ahead of my child's safety. I couldn't be that selfish.

Maybe if my mother had been strong enough to put her children ahead of herself, none of all the horrible things in my life would have happened. Maybe Michael and Devlen wouldn't have been messed up beyond repair.

I couldn't repeat my mother's mistakes. Even if it meant ripping out my own heart instead.

The faint sound of a knock on the front door tore me out of my thoughts.

I swallowed thickly and climbed off the bed, wiping my sweaty palms against my thighs.

There was no more time for thinking. Blaine was here.

HE STOOD JUST inside the front door, arms folded across his leather-clad chest when I came out from the bedroom. Both the twins were talking to him, and from the frown on his face they weren't discussing the weather. Marcus was nowhere in sight.

Blaine looked up as I came around the corner, his frown only deepening as he locked eyes with me.

My heart flip-flopped in my chest at the look in his eyes. It was dark. Yearning.

It made me forget every reservation and every fear I'd had for the past hour. Without thought, I launched myself across the room and into his arms.

The soft leather of his coat pressed against me as he closed his arms around me and lifted me up. I cradled my head against the side of his neck and closed my ankles behind his lower back. My bulging stomach pressed firmly into his, keeping me from getting as close as I needed to be fully secure, but Blaine put a hand underneath my backside and another around my back, supporting my weight perfectly.

He held me close, his head buried in my hair. His breath huffed against the shell of my ear in deep, shaky draws, and I knew he was fighting to stay in control of the onslaught of emotions that currently warred inside my chest, too. It took all I had not to start bawling like a baby.

Home. I was home.

"So... we're gonna head out then," one of the twins said. "Give you two some time to catch up."

They both gave Blaine a pat on the shoulder before they left, leaving us alone in the apartment.

When they were gone, Blaine pulled his head back a

little, and when I looked up, he brushed his mouth gently against mine.

My heart sped up at the tingling spreading in my lips from his featherlight caress. Mindlessly, I tightened my fingers around his shoulders and kissed him back with every ounce of need and every drop of desperation in my body and soul.

Blaine's grip on me tightened as our tongues met, and I moaned with bliss.

Yes, yes! This was right—this was what I needed more than the air in my lungs.

When he finally pulled back, we were both breathing hard.

"Hey," he whispered.

"Hey," I answered, my lips pulling up in an involuntary smile.

Gently, he let me slide down to the floor again, and I winced when my wound made itself known through the haze of bliss. Right. No steamy make-out sessions right after getting shot.

"Does it hurt a lot?"

"Not really. The hospital gave me excellent drugs."

"Hmm," he rumbled, his brows knitting into a frown as he looked down at me. "Don't ever take a bullet for me again."

"I wasn't planning to," I said. "But maybe don't provoke any more crazy men with guns, either."

Blaine made a noncommittal noise.

"So... what now?" I bit my lip as the bliss of being in his embrace slowly withdrew. As good as it had felt to kiss him, and as much as I wanted to just stay in his protective arms forever, reality began to seep through the cracks.

I was still pregnant with a baby who didn't deserve to grow up in the brutal world I had.

He shrugged. "You tell me. You're the one who ran away. What happens next really depends on whether or not you want to stay."

I blinked. "You would let me go?"

"No." Blaine's lips flattened, but he kept his voice calm and business like. "I won't force you to stay as my wife, but I can't let you leave again. It wouldn't be safe. Especially not... with the baby." His eyes flickered to my stomach for the briefest moment, but I saw the yearning in them clear as day.

I swallowed the lump forming in my throat. "It's not that easy, Blaine. I..."

"I love you," he said softly.

"I love you too," I whispered, sniffling. I was quickly losing the battle to the tears. "But I saw you hurt that man. I know you... I know you hurt people all the time. It's what men like you do. And I can't... I can't put my baby through that. I can't hurt it like you and I were hurt by growing up like this."

Blaine reached out and wiped the tears from my cheeks with a thumb. His other hand curved around my belly. "It's *our* baby, love. And I don't want him to grow up like we did, either. I want him to grow up with love and safety. That man you saw me... saw me torture—he was scum. He's kidnapped and brutally raped countless women. But more importantly, he had insider information about your family's connection to the Belfast prostitution ring, and I needed him to tell me so I could nail your father for what he did to you as a kid. Make sure he never walked free again.

"I'm not sorry for what I did to that guy, and I'm not sorry for every sleazeball I'm going to hurt in the future to make sure you're safe. But I will promise you this, Mira: if you stay with me, if you let me be the husband you deserve, I won't hurt anyone who isn't a threat to you or our family. And I will spend every moment of every day worshiping you. You are the only one who has ever made me feel whole—like there is more to me than what my father created with his violence and terror. You are the only one I could ever love. You, and our little one.

"Please, Mira. Please stay with me."

I was crying in earnest now, and no matter how much Blaine stroked at my cheeks, the tears kept coming thick and fast. But despite my outright sobbing, the swell of emotions in my chest were for once strikingly clear.

I had a man who had gone against everything he'd been taught just to make sure I was safe, and who swore to do anything and everything to keep me that way.

A man, who loved me despite everything I'd put him through in my fear.

The only thing I felt as I raised up on my tiptoes and pressed a salty kiss to his lips was happiness so strong it nearly took my breath away.

"Yes," I whispered against his lips. "I will stay with you. Forever and always."

"Blaine!"

I smiled at the irritated voice calling from the nursery. The closer Mira got to her due date, the outright bitchier she was getting, but I didn't mind all that much. Her pregnancy hormones were still ensuring multiple rounds of sex every day, so I took her equally frequent yelling in good spirit.

It was pretty hard to be too upset when you were working on a constant orgasm-high.

I stripped my T-shirt off and jogged up the stairs toward the nursery.

"You called, my beautiful love?" I said with a smirk as I stepped into the room we had both spent so much time picking out furniture and decor for these past few months. I had never been much of an interior designer, to put it mildly, but when it came to our baby's room, I'd found myself having an opinion about cots and lambskin and those colorful things you hang over a baby's crib that I had no idea what was called. I wanted this kid to know he was loved from the moment he opened his eyes.

In the center of the room, with her hands on her round hips, my balloon-shaped wife was standing with an irritated scowl on her face. "You painted it blue! After I specifically said we would go for something gender neutral."

I shrugged and swaggered over to her to put my hands around her face so I could lift her chin and kiss her on the nose.

"Ugh, Blaine, stop that!" she hissed, swatting at my hands as I let them travel down to her full breasts. "They're sore, and I'm mad at you!"

"You're mad at me because I painted the room blue?" I asked innocently, without taking my hands off her tits. I knew how to navigate her pregnancy-swollen body without causing her any discomfort, and I also knew she'd be up for a quick fuck once she was done yelling at me.

"Yes! We don't know the gender, and what if it's a girl?"

"Then she's getting a pretty, robin's egg blue room, Mrs. Shrink. Shouldn't you be all about color-equality? Besides. I have a feeling it's a boy."

Mira's cheeks flushed a pretty pink, and I hid my

smirk against the top of her auburn hair. She didn't particularly like it when I pointed out I had her beat, and I was looking forward to a quick romp before I had to get back to work.

"Yes, well... just because you keep calling the baby 'he' doesn't mean it's a boy."

"Mmhm," I agreed, letting my hands slide underneath her heavy breasts to gently lift them up the way she especially liked after they'd grown two cup sizes with the pregnancy. I loved to feel the weight of them in my hands. Everything about her had always been so lush and beautiful, but seeing her heavy with my child really revved my engine. The twins called me perverted, but I didn't give a fuck. Nothing was sexier than the feel of my pregnant wife underneath and around me.

"I know what you're doing," she grumbled, but the way she tilted her head to give me better access to the sensitive spots on her neck told me she didn't mind in the least.

"You are a smart bird," I hummed into her ear before I obligingly dipped my lips to her throat.

"Jerk," she growled angrily.

"Mmhm." My cock was already hard in my jeans, and I regretted not getting out of them sooner. But when I reached down to undo the zipper, Mira jerked against me.

I looked up from her neck. "You okay, love?"

A pained spasm went across her face, and my heart dropped. Something was wrong.

"Love? Is it the baby?"

Mira breathed deeply a few times before she looked up at me. "Yeah. I think... I think it's time, Blaine."

"What do you mean, 'time'?" I said, doing my best to fight back the rising panic in my gut. I'd left my phone downstairs, so I couldn't call anyone for help. I could always run down the stairs and alert the guys out front, but then I'd have to leave her behind—

"The baby's coming," she interrupted me with an eye roll, seconds before I was about to lift her up and carry her down myself in a full sprint. "Stop panicking and go get my bag. It's time to see if you're right about it being a boy."

I stared at her for a couple of seconds, my mind slowly shaking off the panic.

"It's time?" I said.

Mira smiled, probably at my slow processing. "Yeah, it is. Are you ready?"

Was I ready?

Nine months ago, I would have said no—absolutely was I not ready to be a father, not now, not ever.

But then she had come into my life. My wife. And I had finally learned what it meant to be truly happy.

Starting a family with her... No matter what happened going forward, with my father and our tense truce, with the business and with all the bad blood selling out the Clerys had brought down upon us, I knew it was all worth it. Because I had my own little family now, and no one was ever going to take it away from me.

Yes, I was ready.

MONSTER

Read Marcus' story in *Monster*, book 2 in the Made &
Broken series.

MONSTER

I'll kill to protect her. And then I'll make her mine.

Marcus

They always called me crazy. Sociopath. A monster without a conscience.

I always thought they were right. I've never backed down from anything, and the only thing that has ever soothed the monster in my chest was killing.

Then she walked into my life. The woman who seduced me so she could sell my secrets to my enemy.

I should have killed her, but when I looked into her eyes I knew she was the only one who could save me from myself.

Evelyn

It was supposed to be an easy job: seduce a ruthlessly handsome man and steal his pen drive while he's sleeping. Not the worst thing I've had to do while working for the mafia. By far.

I didn't know Marcus Steel was the son of London's most dangerous crime family—and I didn't know one night with him meant that every criminal in London would be after my blood.

He's the only one powerful enough to protect me

now, but I'm not sure if that's what he's got in mind. I've seen what he does to people who cross him.

He's a monster.

And now, his sights are set on me.

MONSTER - SNIPPET

EVELYN

I knew I was in trouble when my boss didn't send a regular goon to pick me up.

For the first time since I'd made the mistake of borrowing money from Gerald Brigs, casino owner, mafia boss and all-round scumbag, he came by my flat in person. Not a good sign.

In my one and a half years of service to London's underworld, I'd learned that any deviation from the norm was never good.

"Evelyn. Always a pleasure, my dear," said the man on my doorstep. He was wearing a trench coat and a thin-lipped smile that didn't touch his eyes.

I tried to return the expression, but could only manage a grimace as I swept my gaze over his three companions. The two goons he'd brought as bodyguards I didn't recognize, but the third man I did.

Where Gerald rarely bothered with his lowliest employees, his nephew, Leo, was the guy who usually briefed me on my marks and dealt with any situations the goons couldn't. I'd also witnessed what he did to the prostitutes unfortunate enough to work for the Brigs empire. I made it a point to never be alone in a room with him.

"Have I done something wrong?" I asked. Leo closed the door behind the two, leaving their two-goon escort outside. I mentally reviewed the details of the last assignment they'd given me. I had done everything they'd asked, as I always did. I might not have made it to university, but I was smart enough to know what happened to people who disobeyed a crime lord.

"On the contrary," Gerald said as he took in my studio flat. "You've been doing such an excellent job, we've decided it's time to entrust you with something a bit more... delicate." He reached into his coat and produced a brown A4 envelope.

I took the brief from him, examining its contents. Where normally the envelope would contain a couple of pages' worth of information on the mark, this time there was only a picture and a series of seemingly random words. I held it up, scrutinizing it to see what was so different about this guy.

The first thing I noticed was that he was exceedingly handsome. His black hair was tousled perfectly, though it was obvious it had required no effort on his part. Dark brows framed his gray, almond-shaped eyes and his cheekbones were strong and defined. If his mouth hadn't been so soft, his features would almost have been too prominent to call beautiful. But it was—and he looked like a freaking supermodel.

"Er... are you sure I'm a good match?" I bit my lip, feeling oddly self-conscious under the intensity of the photo's stare. "I mean..."

It wasn't that I was bad-looking. My figure might have been fuller than what was considered the hallmark of conventional beauty, but my curves had lured enough hapless men into Brigs' claws that I knew the appeal of my red hair, round hips, and full breasts. But this guy was clearly a class—or five—above mine. I was distinctly more girl-next-door than swimsuit model.

"I mean, he's probably used to more high society girls," I finally managed, pulling my gaze from the picture to look at my boss.

A small smile pulled on his lips. "You're the perfect girl for this job. His name is Marcus Steel, and he has something of mine. A pen drive. I want you to get an invitation to his flat and find this pen drive for me. It's bound to be somewhere secure, so there's a chance you'll have to get into his safe. The list on there are things and people that might mean something to him. Use that to work out the code."

I blinked down at the list. "How on Earth am I meant to figure out a code to his safe from random words?" I might have plenty of street smart, but solving ciphers was above my pay grade.

Brigs' smile turned cooler. "Don't sell yourself short. We've been nothing but pleased with your results so far —I am certain you won't disappoint me this time, either. After all, such a *delicate* assignment will cut a thousand pounds off your debt rather than the usual five hundred."

His tone made it clear that I didn't want to find out what would happen if I failed. Then the other implied part of the assignment dawned on me and I paled. I had lured men with the promise of my body before, but I'd never had to follow through. Once the poor idiots followed me to the designated drop-off point, Brigs' goons had always taken over. But if I was supposed to get an invitation to this mark's home... then there would be no one to intervene. And a guy like that would most definitely expect sex if he brought a woman home.

It was kind of funny—before Brigs, I would have been more than happy to spend a night with a man that looked like this Marcus Steel, but now... When Brigs had discussed how I could repay my loan, I'd been very adamant I wouldn't work in one of his brothels, which was what landed me my job as a Honey Trap. But deep down, I'd known it would only be a matter of time before they would make me go all the way.

The way Leo treated the other women in his employ, it was pretty obvious no one in the Brigs empire cared about a woman's right to her own body.

I dug my nails into the palm of my free hand. I knew better than to protest. I'd just have to work out how to get out of any sexual obligations once I was inside Marcus Steel's home. I might be forced to work for the mafia, but someday I would be free from them again, and when that day came I wanted to be able to look myself in the eye.

I forced a smile on my face as I looked at my boss. "Okay. I'll get your pen drive back. Where can I find this Marcus Steel?"

ELEONORE WAS one of the fanciest clubs I'd ever been to. I picked up my marks at clubs often enough, but they were usually the type with loud dance music and a mixture of drugs and semen lining the bathroom stalls.

When I walked up to *Eleonore*, the red carpet guiding the way to the doors muted the sound of my clicking heels, and instead of jarring dubstep blasting out whenever a patron passed through the double doors, the soft, lilting notes of jazz music wafted into the night.

I smiled hesitantly at the huge bouncer taking up most of the step in front of the door. Even though I'd worn the kind of camouflage that would help me fit in here—a black dress that managed to still look classy, even though it certainly marketed my cleavage nicely—I didn't exactly feel at home. Even when I wasn't working for Brigs, my usual attire consisted of jeans and a t-shirt. Or, of course, my uniform when I worked my day job as a waitress. *Eleonore* managed to make me feel like I was sticking out like a sore thumb before I'd even gotten inside.

But the bouncer simply unclipped the red velvet rope for me, stepping aside as he let me through.

"Thank you," I said as I passed him, offering him a smile as well.

If he heard me, he ignored me. *Well, suit yourself, Grumpy.*

I left my coat with a girl working the wardrobe and continued in through another set of double doors, these ones made from glass with gilded bars functioning as door knobs.

I had to pull myself together to not let my jaw hit my chest at the barrage of impression that washed over me on the other side. At the far corner was a beautiful bar, which looked like it was made from hardwood and polished so perfectly even the soft lighting in the club reflected off it. The plush, deep-red carpet from the entrance and corridor turned to parquet flooring that led to multiple high tables and chairs in front of a small dance floor and a stage. Not many people graced the chairs—it was a Tuesday night, after all—but on the stage a band played the enticing jazz rhythms I'd been able to hear since entering the club.

I soaked in the atmosphere, enjoying the sophisticated ambience as much as the music itself. I'd always loved jazz.

But I was here for a job, and it didn't involve standing around wishing for things to have worked out differently. I sighed, pulling myself out of the revelry.

A quick scan of the few patrons at the tables told me that my mark wasn't among them, nor was he part of one of the two couples slow dancing in front of the stage, seemingly lost to the rest of the world. Thank God. That could have been awkward.

I looked back over at the bar and frowned at the flirting couple near the end closest to me. They were blocking my view of the other side of it, so I decided to walk on over and check it out. If nothing else, a drink was always a good way to calm my nerves before I picked up my mark.

On the other side of the couple, a tall man sat at the very far end, one shoulder leaned against the wall. My heart sped up with a burst of adrenaline. Could it be him? I craned my neck in an effort to see him better, but he was facing away. All I could see was ebony hair and incredibly wide shoulders underneath a black shirt.

"What can I get you, miss?"

I jolted at the unexpected voice and flashed a nervous smile at the barman. Something about the underplayed extravagance set me on edge, as if everyone would be able to tell I came from several rungs down the social ladder.

"Vodka and tonic, thanks," I said, trying to keep my tone indifferent and effortless.

When he grabbed for the bottle of Grey Goose, I had to bite the inside of my cheek to keep from protesting. Instead, I smiled sweetly when he passed me my drink and added a generous tip. Brigs always covered expenses, and if Tall, Dark, and Mysterious at the end of the bar didn't turn out to be Marcus Steel, then I might need the barman's help to locate him later.

Mustering my courage, I took a quick sip of my drink and then walked over to the seat right next to the guy I was hoping was my mark.

"It's a lovely band," I said as I slid in on the bar stool, somehow managing to get on it relatively gracefully. Being a short girl doesn't make wrangling of bar stools an easy task.

Talk, Dark, and Mysterious didn't so much as spare me a glance.

Maybe he didn't hear me?

"Do you come here often?" Okay, so it was cheesy, but from my experience, it worked.

His only reaction was to take a swig of what looked like cola from his own glass.

Right, then. So he was an arse. I pinched my lips and reminded myself I preferred it that way—my job was better when the guy Brigs had me lure into a trap was a jerk. It made it easier to pretend like he deserved what happened to him after I left him with Brigs' goons.

Emboldened by my annoyance, I skipped past the usual smalltalk and instead slipped my drink-free hand underneath the bar and onto his thigh, letting my finger-tips graze the bulge between them.

The strength of his muscles clenching underneath my touch surprised me—I could *feel* the power in his thigh against my palm and half-expected him to shoot out of his chair.

It wasn't what I'd expected. Surprise, sure, but the deathly silence from my unwilling companion made an eerie sense of foreboding tingle down my spine and raise every hair on my body. Slowly, I looked up, my irritation with his previous lack of response replaced by anxiety.

Marcus Steel's ice-gray eyes met mine when my gaze made it all the way up.

Only the man staring down at me was nothing like his picture. Sure, his ruthless good looks were the same, from the black cascade of tousled hair to the soft lips and defined features, but what was *behind* that icy gaze, the photo hadn't managed to convey. If it had, I would have tried much, much harder to get out of this assignment.

Everything about that look screamed *danger*, making

the reptilian part of my brain wake in a shock of adrenaline.

I trembled as every nerve ending strained to its fullest, making my skin so hypersensitive I could feel the warmth radiating from him. The faint trace of his cologne hit my flared nostrils, along with something else. Something unidentifiable that heated the lower parts of my abdomen and made me squeeze my thighs together, even as a primal fear dug its claws in deep.

Oh. Maybe "*it*" wasn't so unidentifiable, after all.

There was no doubt in mind, after no more than three seconds' eye contact, that this man was trouble.

But he was also one hundred percent alpha male, and despite the overwhelming sense of peril that rushed over me staring into his eyes, my body was seemingly also perfectly in tune with the *other* aspect of his nature.

The unexpected flood of arousal dampened my initial fear enough that I remembered I probably needed to say something soon.

"Hi," I croaked. Not the smoothest of lines, but given how my hand was still grasping his thigh, too petrified to let go, I figured it was better than nothing.

Marcus didn't respond, and his face remained completely impassive.

"I'm Evelyn Embry," I continued, my voice still not much louder than a hoarse whisper. The second my name left my lips I could have smacked myself. I hadn't meant to give him my real name—it was page-freaking-one in dealing with a mark. But his overwhelming presence had made it slip out without conscious thought, and now there was nothing I could do to take it back. Hopefully, he would have forgotten it before he ever realized my true intentions.

His eyes finally moved then, flicking briefly to my hair, across my face and—finally—to my amply displayed breasts, where they lingered for just a second before he looked back up again. His gaze made a hot blush follow the path of his eyes, and I couldn't hold back a shaky exhale as I stared into his darkened eyes. His pupils seemed larger, as if the light in the room had dimmed, even though the shine from the polished bar told me otherwise.

"What you're selling, little sister, I'm not buying."

I blinked at the rumbling timbre of his voice. The softness in it completely contradicted everything else about his presence.

"I'm not selling anything."

His eyes briefly landed on my hand on his thigh. My fingertips were still brushing ever so lightly against the bulge of his cock.

"*Oh!* No, I'm not... I'm not a prostitute," I stammered, my blush increasing ten-fold. Yeah, of course he would think the stranger groping him would be looking for a client. *Eleonore* wasn't your run-of-the-mill nightclub—uninvited touching wasn't expected.

This wasn't working out at all like I'd planned. I

finally managed to remove my hand from his thigh, placing it awkwardly on the bar between us.

"I just..." I looked up into those glacier-cool eyes and felt all my barriers come crumbling down. How did a single person shake me so thoroughly? I felt naked underneath his stare, and it both frightened and aroused me more than it had any business doing. "I wanted to meet you."

"Why?"

Not the question I'd expect from a guy who looked like Marcus Steel.

"You're the most handsome man I've ever seen." I frowned. "Why do women normally want to meet you?"

His face remained impassive, but the darkness in his eyes intensified, pulling at those warring sensations in my gut: the cold dread of adrenaline, and the hot, champagne fizz of pure sexual attraction. "They don't."

I raised both eyebrows. "I find that really hard to believe."

Finally, he turned away from me, relegating his full focus to his glass as he took a swig. "They're scared of me."

Well, that I could believe. I looked back at my own drink, mulling over my plan of attack. Now that he wasn't staring at me so intensely, I could think clearly again—even if every cell of my body was still keenly aware of his proximity.

"*I* want to know you," I said, glancing out the corner of my eye for a reaction.

Marcus put his glass down, still not looking in my direction.

"You're scared of me, too." The deep rumble in his voice sent shivers up my back. If he knew I was flirting, he wasn't responding. But he wasn't ignoring me, either.

"Yes," I said, deciding honesty was my best course with this man. Gently, I placed my hand back on top of his thigh, a bit lower this time. Again, he tensed at my touch, but not as rigidly as before.

"But that doesn't change the fact that I want you more than I've ever wanted another man in my life." I glanced up at his profile, flustered by the knowledge that this wasn't just a line delivered to ensnare a mark, nor was it a lie. "Maybe that's what scares me."

He looked at me then, and this time, the darkness in his eyes bore the faintest trace of heat. But it wasn't the kind of lust I'd seen in a man's eyes before. It was far more volatile, far more frightening than anything I'd known before, and even the barest hint of his desire set my body aflame with unrivaled *need*.

"No, *Evelyn*. That's not why you're afraid."

"Is it because you'd try to hurt me?" I whispered, my voice breaking.

His nostrils pulled up, a flash of anger mixing with the heat in his gaze. "No."

A breath of relief I hadn't realized I'd been holding

rushed out of my lungs. I believed him. I had no idea what it was about him, but something at the very depths of my being knew he wasn't lying. I grasped my drink and downed the rest of the glass in one, burning mouthful. Then I slid off my seat and stood to face him on shaky legs.

"Come."

Despite the minimal movement of his mouth, I recognized his question in the gesture.

"You're taking me to your place." I slipped my hand from his thigh up to his arm, resting it on the soft fabric of his shirt. "And then you'll let me get to know you."

The slightest crease appeared between his dark eyebrows, his gaze flickering to my hand on his arm before he found my eyes once more. The desire in his own was more prominent now, and I had to clench my thighs together to quell the sudden rush of warmth blooming out from between them. God, I wanted him. In that moment, I didn't care about my assignment or Brigs or any of the shit I was mixed up in that'd landed me here. I didn't even care that that barely bridled ferocity in his icy gaze flamed as he looked me over once more, taking in my curves as well as my face.

"You don't know what you're asking for," he rumbled.

"Then show me," I said, swallowing thickly as he stared me down.

Marcus exhaled through his nose. Then, moving as

smoothly as a large cat, he got off the chair and held his hand out to me.

Gingerly, I put my palm in his.

When he closed his hand around mine, I knew I would never be the same as I had been before I met Marcus Steel.

Continue reading in
MONSTER

ALSO BY NORA ASH

MADE & BROKEN SERIES

Dangerous

Monster

Trouble

DEMON'S MARK SERIES

Branded

Demon's Mark

Prince of Demons

FERAL SERIES

Obsession

Despair

Torment

ALPHA SERIES

Taken

Masquerade

Mated

THE OMEGA PROPHECY

Ragnarök Rising

Weaving Fate

ANCIENT BLOOD SERIES

Origin

Wicked Soul

Debt of Bones*

DARKNESS SERIES

Into the Darkness

Hidden in Darkness

Shades of Darkness

Fires in the Darkness

WWW.NORA-ASH.COM

www.ingramcontent.com/pod-product-compliance
Lightning Source LLC
Chambersburg PA
CBHW050819190726
48286CB00007B/1921